THE SNOWS OF HELICON

THE SNOWS OF HELICON

By

H. M. TOMLINSON

HARPER & BROTHERS PUBLISHERS

New York and London

1933

THE SNOWS OF HELICON

Copyright, 1933, by H. M. Tomlinson

Printed in the United States of America

First Edition

G-H

To

Susan and Nicholas

THE SNOWS OF HELICON

Chapter One

A LONG ARRAY OF DECK-CHAIRS WAS RECESSED ON THE promenade deck of the *Cambodia*. That liner's deck was as broad as a town's thorofare. The resting passengers slept, or read, or stared into the outer bright void; and with their heads at that moment a trifle lower than their heels. Travers opened his eyes, blinking drowsily, and thought they were filmed; he wondered whether anything had happened to his sight. He took a steadier look at the void.

His eyes were all right, but there was no sea. Sea and clouds had gone. The ship had run into a drift of fog-banks. The Atlantic and the sky were veiled in invisible gauze. The substantial wooden rail of the bulwarks, and the stanchions, were the final outliers of reality. Nothing was beyond them, or only a vast translucency, with no ocean, and no heaven; though the sun, which also had vanished, had not gone very far. It was blazing unseen in space from which sea and sky were expunged.

I

The roll of the steamer reversed at leisure. The straight line of the bulwarks descended the brightness till Travers saw scattered crescents of burnished water, apparently at varying levels, and the phantom glow of the wake of the hidden sun streaming from beneath a sightless curtain of mist. He eyed in contentment the vague apparition of reality beyond the security of the deck. He felt there was nothing significant in wraiths, not even in the faint wraith of the Atlantic. His problems were suspended. He could not see them. They were with him, but retired and improbable.

Maybe that young deck steward had something to do with it. There he was then. He was gazing, as if it pleased him, at the glinting of a sun-track from no visible sun. Broad swells pulsed under the haze. When that chap appeared, and began hovering about the chairs cumbering an uncertain deck, he was more notable, Travers thought, than the fine people he served. He was a Cockney only when he spoke. His speech was part of his disguise, like his white jacket. What was he before he was a steward, or between his hours of service? There was a touch of derision in his politeness; anyhow, there was if you felt sulky. That delicacy and deference rebuked. And they annoyed. A man who had the job of handing round plates ought not to do it as though you were forgiven. Even that budding but already jaded woman, that girl who honoured the ship by merely showing herself on deck, with her haughty languor which told everybody how tedious these surroundings were, when she happened to notice them, even she treated that steward as if he were a human being. He had been dodging about the chairs just before, with his beastly tea and biscuits, as Travers was dozing—for it wasn't easy to sleep at night, when the mind went clear and steady in solitude, and the drone of the ship was the undertone of the universe on its way. Travers had to rouse himself, saw it was only teacups and the deck steward, and shook his head.

Then for a dull minute he watched the little fellow, standing by the side of the chair where the disdainful nymph reclined in the Hollywood notion of Aspasia, a few steps aft. Beyond the steward was the afternoon brightness of nothing in particular, that dazzling shimmer of the speed of their progress. Queer! Perhaps it was a trick of the light. The chap was floating over them, superior through a slow heave of the ship. He was smiling down at the lady, as in an assurance that he was there by chance, and would not intrude for

3

more than a moment. He was much too high-born to show that he was anything but a servant; yet he had forgotten the glory about his fair head. The light was entangled with it.

Travers admired, and pondered sleepily. Where had he seen a face like that before? When was it? It must have been that spring, when he was sketching at Syracuse. That was long ago. And that was the head of a goatherd. Here was a liner, in the later days, and a steward. In that quivering opaline glow identities were fused. There was no past. There was only an abiding present.

Somebody was laughing. Hullo! The sea certainly had a big broad back to it, though it had disappeared. His chair was rising; it was of no weight; it was getting off the deck. His body had lost its ballast. It was warm there in the lee, almost as genial as Sicily in spring, when you saw the fountain of Arethusa for the first time, and the ancient temples by the deserted shore at Selinunte. Ah, that Ionian coast! What a difference between being young in Sicily, with all to do, though you didn't know what, and a famous architect building for people for whom beauty and the Greeks had gone to sere stalks of caraway and broken marble on a shore that was forgotten! Well astern now, that

4

country. Forgotten. No Phidias was needed, not when all that was asked for was whacking great containers of concrete and steel. Still, you could do a scrap of relief with a colonnade of red and green petrol pumps.

Now there were two of those stewards. Where had the other fellow come from? That was the Sicilian chap. It was a new uniform they were wearing; they were good, too, those tunics and girdles. The two of them were mighty serious, as they gazed down into that bright deep. The deck was cleared of chairs. Nobody else was about. Those two stewards were off duty. It was a terrific drop, over the ship's side. There below was the outline of America. The shape was plain enough, in the markings of a distant globe. No mistaking the Gulf of Mexico and Hudson Bay, even when all that way down. What could they see down there, those two? Nothing could be made out on that great moon, sunk far in the air.

Steward! No answer. They couldn't hear him. It was too quiet, where they were. Steward! Very likely they couldn't see him. They took no notice of him. It was risky, moving about at that height, when you were no better than a feather, to float off over nothing.

That Cockney, that fair fellow, was telling his

brother a tale. He was pointing down to the pale globe, and he had a long yarn about it. You could not hear him with the light so dazzling, but there was no need. Those two fellows must be nearer the sun, to shine like that. They were gods. That was why they were tranquil and bright. One was pointing below. He had something to do. He ought to go. Nothing had been given to that place for too long. Not a word had been sent to it since it was young. If it were left to itself much longer then they might as well aim a comet at it and finish it. It was sour and smoky. It was restless and cruel. It would be past help soon, the way it was going. They ought never to have left a half-word with those wingless and mortal sons of time, a glimpse at what was hidden, and then abandoned them to their own devices with it. Poor sport, that! See what had happened to men, through whispering so much to them, yet not enough! The ingenious creatures had worked so hard with the hint that they were doomed now, unless they were given more light. There should be another word, a full word, to change their minds, to release them from the spell.

The dark fellow was laughing at his brother. What was there to do? That sphere was new—it had been alive only since yesterday—it would eclipse when it

had made its circle, then out would go its nonsense.
As if the full word could be used where light came
only for a day! What could be done with it in a day?
Those parodies of gods below were quite well as they
were. It wasn't a little day to them. It was a splendid
conquest. They were overcoming the elements. They
were conquering nature. They enjoyed themselves
as gods with the wrong half of a word. They were
having a hearty lark with it. Why spoil their pleasure?
And what fun it was to watch them, especially as the
best of them grew quite dangerous once in a while—
nearly chanced on the right answer—almost turned the
key! But the wrong guess pleased most of them much
more. It happened to give them what they wanted.
So why should they hear any new word, if they were
not listening for it, and wouldn't rejoice if they heard
it? Leave them alone. They'd care nothing for anything he said, in the triumphant din of the excitement
they loved. Let them scuttle about. What cruelty, to
worry them with a rumour of what they could not
see! Why, the row they made gave them the confidence to tell each other they were the sons of God.
What more could they have? And what a mortal fool
he'd look, if he told them he was the driver of the
chariot of the sun! How they'd laugh! They'd tie him

7

to an iron wheel of their own, and bid him prove his word. Now drive that!

The dark lad was laughing. He gave his brother a playful shove. He pushed him over in merriment. Then go! Get on with it! The bright lad floated off, and sank.

Chapter Two

TRAVERS STRUGGLED TO RISE. HE WANTED TO GET TO
the bulwarks to see, but he could not move. The ship
soared against him; the radiance dimmed.

He must have been asleep. The Cockney steward
was solicitous. He was helping Travers out of the huddle into which the roll of the ship had flung him.
Travers peered round and up at the little man, unbe-
lievingly, trying to get him into his rightful place. The
sun had gone. That fellow had fallen a long way, in a
few seconds. That word! What was that word?

"You were in a deep sleep, sir!"

Travers thanked him, smiling back. A deep sleep,
was it! Or was the steward discreet? The idea of that
discretion amused the passenger. No good asking a
steward for such a word. Better not try it on. Maybe
it could not be trusted to the likes of him. And if you
don't know the right word then you wouldn't understand it if you heard it. He had been very near to
knowing it at last, all the same. He should have slept

9

on for another minute. The ship had rolled at an unlucky instant. Could it reverse, and put him back where he had been? No; not after you are awake. When you are awake, there you are, and you have to admit it. How to awake from that? You are never in doubt that you are awake; and then the gods are dead.

He glanced along the deck. Most of the chairs were empty. It was chilly. This was the last night of the voyage. Tomorrow, Liverpool. There it would start. This little interlude was nearly over, and when it was the infernal racket would break out again, the old shattering uproar, common-sense baffled in its yearning to escape from it, to be able to stand still long enough to notice the pattern of the sunlight. No chance of that. It was about to begin again, the absorbing consideration of material and its qualities, its stresses and strains, tensions and torsions, all to be related and poised, adjustments and compensations so calculated that nobody would question the imposing result. That was good fun, too, when the shape embodied the idea. But when it only satisfied the megalomania of barbarians you were only piling up lumber.

Now he had to do that new London hotel. It would be wonderful. Its fabulous cost would justify it. Who would have the nerve to doubt the loudest and most extravagant thing ever done? That was the stuff to give them. Nobody supposed that anything but benefit could come of what was elephantine and costly. The greater buildings which arose because material desires enlarged with the quickening rhythm of life always did look as though they never could topple. They were rightly set to the nicer calculations of science, which was always ready to gratify desire. They were from everlasting to everlasting. Everybody banked on them and in them. They towered ever higher and spread ever farther. They were prodigious. They had audacious and conquering severity, as though their foundations were sunk in the rock of ages and their parapets true to the aligning finger of God. What but money's worth could ever come from them? Good old towers of Babel! He went down to his cabin.

There he found Mantell. That cheered Travers. He liked that young fellow. That youth—from both Oxford and Harvard, which seemed rather like overdoing culture—was the giddy scoffer to hearten a senior duffer who had underslept himself; who had lost his dream. Mantell knew what to say about dreams to anyone incapable of blushing. That boy had doubts, too, but he managed to get plenty of fun out of them. He was only positive when in doubt. Blue devils arranged into a giddy ballet for him. He made them dance the hula-hula. To him it was a comic suggestion that all our great doings were sure to go stiff in an eternal solar frost, some day. Travers chuckled. There was nothing of your bilious gloom about these modern sceptics. They grabbed hold of the barbed tail and tickled the Satanic nose with it. Clapped a bowler hat on the respectable horns of that doddering old bungler at sin.

"There you are, my lad!"

"Hullo, Travers!"

Mantell took his feet from the edge of Travers' bed, flung a book on it, and unrolled his long limbs. He stood, and reduced the size of the cabin. He was grinning. "I say, Travers, you have got some gummy books here. Do you toy with Buddhism? Won't it send you potty?"

Travers continued to survey his visitor in satiric silence.

"I say," continued Mantell, "I've barged in. Sorry. I want you to dine with me tonight."

The elder man sat down. He indulged in the relief afforded to a misgiving heart by the buoyancy of rebellious and healthy youth.

"Don't say no. I want to talk. I'm starving for want

of a talk. And its your last chance to see us, you know. My saloon has the only real people in the ship. I've told you so before, but you wouldn't listen. Eh? You've no idea what you miss. There's a guy at my table, wears half-a-pint of diamonds, too, a sort of white man, nationality unknown, and he eats grape-fruit with a fish-knife. What, haven't you seen it done? Certainly. It's quite easy, when you know the way. You load a juicy section on it, and incline the knife like a gangplank. Then you slide up the fruit with the right forefinger. He hardly ever misses. If you are diet-ing, you don't have to eat at my table. You only have to watch."

Travers doubted. He fancied the surgeon was ex-pecting him.

"That's not right. Let him wait. Don't do it. He'd only give you bacteria and the world crisis. They'll do fine. Leave trypanosomes and peace propaganda alone for one evening. They'll get there just the same."

The elder man made no sign. Mantell paused, and then pleaded further. "Come along. I say, you're a democrat, ain't you? So you've said. Isn't it time you learned something of Demos? Come and eat with the mob. You build your picture-palaces for it, don't you? Then you ought to look at it for once, and thankfully, dammit. . . . Yes, you have. You've got time all right. You've been with the tourist people more than is good for you this voyage. I've noticed it. But they only make things worse. You know what they are, professors and students—like me—going to study the works of mankind; for a holiday, too. They only clot your warm juices with more cold intellect than is good for any sane man. Come along, Travers. I know you want to fly from the first saloon, because you can't eat in comfort with the dead. They've made good, your crowd—they've come to the end of thanksgiving. Like you. You have, haven't you? Only you hate being dead. My crowd is hairy. That's where the good red stuff is, all warm and flowing, and no constipating thought about it. Come along. . . . No, that's all right. You don't have to dress to-night."

Travers continued in cordial abstraction, listening with but one ear, to regard his visitor. This youngster was real, not in the least vaporous. Nothing ambiguous about him. Perhaps he was right. Travers knew that though he himself was of importance in his profession, he did not live in Whitman's world of the modern, even though he gave it picture-palaces and hotels; he had lapsed into the notion that the exciting present had little to do with him, hardly more than the late

activities of the Toltecs. The whole tumultuous spec-
tacle whirled in another dimension; he was in a calm
apart. A dead calm. A vacuum? His habit was to look
distantly at the flux of mankind. He never picked up
one of its newspapers without expectation, and always
put it down in astonishment and alarm. It looked ugly.
Would that threatening multitude ever sweep in over
him? A disturbing thought, that. It could come cruelly
close. Sometimes, in the street, he met its eyes, the direct stare of that other life, the antipathy of an unknown body in ambush, a lithe but heavy creature of
overwhelming force and cunning. It was wiser to keep
out of its way.

"No, not to-night, Mantell. I want . . . well, I
shouldn't enjoy myself if I came."

"What you want is a bracer. You've forgotten how
to enjoy yourself. Come and pick it up again. I know
what's wrong with you fastidious people. You don't
want to believe that a dollop of original mud makes
a soul more lifelike and lovable. But what's the good
of a soul without mud in it? Do you know, in my
saloon, any meal-time, there's Poles and Jews and
Slovenes, there's most of the brands of the old marl
of Europe, the real rough stuff, as good as the day it
was mixed. Swine-herds and goose-girls. You'd like

them. They make fashionable beauties look no warmer than draper's models, nothing but face. There's an old Jew sits near me, and I think he's Moses, just down from Pisgah. He wears a high hat at dinner. The life in our saloon is laval, Travers, out of the bowels of the earth."

"I don't care much for the bowels of the earth. Let me see. Now I think of it, I've hardly spoken to any-one but yourself since I came aboard. I'd sooner be alone. The first morning out was the only time I went the length of the deck. I wanted companionship; without knowing what I wanted, very likely. I'll give you that much. I saw here and there a face which I thought might prove friendly, if I could make—how shall I put it?—the right signal. But I fancied I wasn't seen. I couldn't think of a signal, either. I'm afraid I don't know the signs."

"What of it? You'd soon learn them. They're easy. Who knows? Why, one of the more attractive dar-lings might hug you, after you'd made a nice sign, and there you sit, and won't make any signal to life."

"I know. But I'm content, with what I have."

"You're unnaturally selfish. I think your content is just beastly cruelty. All jolly fine to deny life to your-self, if you don't want it, but don't you think it is

16

pretty awful for other people to see you ignore their attractions? Your notions would stagnate the fountain head, turn it green and dry it up, if you left them lying near it."

They went out together, to make their way forward. Mantell guided. "No. Not that way. You don't know your own ship. Down here."

Travers at once began to feel as though he were in another liner. He had that sense of insecurity which came over him when he turned to the newspapers, in a morning light, after a quiet evening with his books. All was confused again, following that confident midnight fancy that he had seen the crooked made straight and the rough places plain.

They passed people he had never seen before, in corridors he did not know existed. The great ship had mysterious extensions, perhaps, and new travellers came every day, as though their vessel were incontinent and had no circumference. Anything was possible, even in a ship. No book could hold it. Strange stewards stood sentinel at corners, and stared at them, as at newcomers. There were unexpected dimensions, foreign smells, and shocking colours. Travers surrendered to the unforeseen. Perhaps it is better to admit you never know where you are, but will try to find out, when you happen to be driven to it. He remembered his first morning aboard. He told Mantell that he had tried to reach the open air before breakfast, but could not find it. No sky was about. So he returned to his cabin, and rang his bell. Steward, where's the sea gone? Show me the sea! I want to look at it!

"The steward shot me up in a lift, dodged round corners, hurried under glazed domes, pushed through doors, and there the sea was, after all. This great engine has no bottom that we know of, and a top only now and then, and goodness knows where the corridors go. I can't see how the puzzle hangs together."

"What does it matter if you can't? All you want is faith; then you can enjoy yourself, without worrying about the bottom. Don't ask questions, and you'll get to Liverpool. A bottom must be somewhere, because here we walk about. Between ourselves, I expect there's poor devils on the lower-most gratings now, holding us up on the way to dinner. We needn't worry because we never see them. They're there, sweating in the bilges, without doubt. If we don't see them we needn't fret about them." Mantell chuckled. "I think we should just take whatever is next to us, if its worth having, and never bother about how it all hangs together. It'll do that, unless the ever-glorious boilers fall through some day. You'd never guess how much does hang together here, either. Do you see that saloon?"

Travers glanced through the curtained window of a seclusion beside them. There, in an interior and subdued light, its origin concealed, a number of ladies, as still as figures in the past, sat intent before antique writing-tables. A fire glowed illusively at one end of the room. It was a retired and illuminated silence, as if Mantell had conjured a peep at a boudoir in old Paris with a sudden nudge.

"See that room? One morning I was passing it, and politely did not look in, because it is not reserved for men. And, as it happened, I wasn't looking for her just then. Then I noticed it was full of sheiks. Certainly. Full of 'em, almost. Arabs of the desert in their robes. I thought that if they were in the ladies' room it gave me a right to stop. After a bit I saw what it was. They were Levites. They were in the vestments of Jerusalem's temple, sir, funny hats and all, and they were solemnly adoring a bulkhead of a room reserved for ladies in the Atlantic. Jerusalem the golden is all about us. Jehovah reigns, I can tell you. As I turned away, there beside me was that gigantic negro prize-fighter we've got aboard. He was staring in. He was so overcome that he had forgotten to smoke his cigar. He was holding it away from his open mouth. 'Say, boss, what's them guys doin', huh?' he asked me.

"What were they doing? That's all the negro wanted to know, only that. Travers, what were they doing?"

Chapter Three

THEY BOTH HESITATED AT THE DOOR OF THE SALOON, forgetful at once of the problem which had astonished even a negro. It left them. A quiet interval from which to discern what men are doing rarely opens around. None was offered then, to plumb to the depth of so queer an Atlantic mystery, because from an alcove of palms issued the caterwauling and clashing of saxophones and tympani, to greet the two friends with musical insults on their approach to dinner. As civilized men, accustomed to a continuance of events and crises apparently as unrelated as flotsam in a tideway, they accepted as somehow inevitable whatever should come next in the flow of progress. The blatant derision of that wayside music checked their impulse to resolve a previous surprise. Our many wonders are passed in neglect. Patient stewards, inured to it, put them in their allotted seats.

Travers took a shy survey of the great apartment. He had not known, from his place in the ship, that this saloon and its company were making the same voyage. He saw that he was lost in it. One more there was no more. In so spacious a hall, and in the midst of that busy and hearty concourse, he did not count. Mantell was in whispered jocular converse with an appreciative steward; he settled himself, and then turned to Travers, making a slight introductory sweep with his hand.

"There it is. There's the multitude. And seeing the multitude, what about it?"

His guest became bolder in a more leisured survey, without adding anything to his knowledge. Demos might be more difficult to play with than Hydra. In that unexpected expansion of the ship there was a confusion of tongues, yet a suggestion of confident ownership and control, and bursts of capricious music, and occasional laughter, and a candid illumination, which did not accord with the feeling of deep waters sweeping under all. A tremor from the hidden power which kept everybody speeding one way through the night came suddenly into the arms of Travers' seat, and his own arms then trembled in involuntary response to the unknown.

"Don't say you don't like it, Mr. Architect. You really looked then as if you were going to run away.

Have something to eat first. . . . I hear you are going to do another marvellous job for us. Hang on a bit, and tell me all about that. Is it another picture-palace, or a new and nobler Billingsgate? Oh, but you are! I've heard about it. I saw it announced in the wireless news yesterday. You don't know you are famous. You're going home to raise topless towers for us somewhere. What are they for?"

The architect remembered his cherished drawings, with private and wry amusement. They had become indistinct and trivial. He recalled a few details which had taken up his time, for he had thought they were good. They were of more importance to him than the form of the building itself, because that was a necessity imposed from without. There was that notion he had outlined for the decoration of the lounge, something busy visitors might notice, if they became listless, and open to impressions through being kept waiting too long. It might sink in then.

Would it? He faltered as he considered that noisy and varied company, which concentrated all Europe and North America. He began to lose faith, too, in the idea of humanity's brotherhood; perhaps a similar bony framework didn't make men alike. The idea that there is only one species of modern man might have nothing in it. Looking about him, he thought it possible that there were more and deeper differences in that ship's company than among those lower creatures which compel separate apartments in a menagerie. He mentioned his doubt to his host.

"More differences? You're right. My word! I should say there are. That's where Buddha and the improvers make their great mistake. They think we're one. The blue-bottomed monkeys never make that mistake about the red. You ought to know that you've about as much relationship with most of the crowd here eating the same food as a robin-redbreast with a crocodile. There's just one thing that unites the lot of us—we easily take fright. Rouse our fears and we're human."

"Nothing to be done for us, then, except to frighten us?"

"Surely you've noticed it?—funk makes brothers of us all. . . . But there isn't anything you want to do for us, is there? We're feeling fine."

"I haven't anything in mind."

"That's really the sensible way to look at it. Don't let us try to think of anything. Nobody would have it, unless he could bask in it."

Travers considered that hope, while noting the opulence of a young woman at a neighbouring table. Her colouring and self-possession reminded him of an amiable lioness. He guessed she was a sandy-haired descendant of the worshippers of Odin. She could bear cuirass and helm nobly, as well as children. Compared with the original sap and essence of such a woman, wasn't his art as inconsequential as a parlour-game? As he watched her, she kindly wiped her fork with her fingers to spear cleanly a roll of bread which a neighbour had begged, an act performed, her body being what it was, with the grace of a monarch giving the accolade. Beside her sat a venerable Israelite, who was not eating, but who was statuesque, his eyes sternly fixed on a verity in mid-air known only to himself; he was above food; there were grey curls pendent on his haggard cheeks and an antique silk hat on his head. Near him was a matron, probably from the real Bohemia, from a primitive and tonic earth where the wilting drugs of culture are unknown. She overlapped a seat built for an inferior base. Her broad face, seamed by experience and weather, was of unctuous brown leather, her expressionless eyes were black. Her hair was kept by a taut orange scarf, and she devoured an impaled sausage, section by section, staring in dull interest round the room after each convincing bite.

Travers warmed to these figures, as each became distinguished, though the incoherent scene itself was ominous. These single human forms, though as unconscious of merit as a flexuous leopard of the disdain in its unrest, were enough to make an impressionable man glad to be alive. And wasn't that enough? An artist knew it was. It was ample, if not all. He could create something from it which was not, till he gave the word. He could justify it. It was good. The earth was young and vivid, it was all a-growing and a-blowing; and time was irrelevant, for it was merely one's own age, it was only the wrinkling of one's own skin.

Yet he was unsatisfied. Did his doubt come of his years? Perhaps his doubt was the inevitable chill beginning to slow his heart. He wondered whether his hesitation before responding to the unconscious flush and dance of life, his reluctance to cheer a luscious scene, was a sign that he was on his way out of it. Who could tell him? The curves of the body and the glow and drive of the blood, contour and dye and movement, still delighted him, yet not as before. He could not move at once in glad and necessary response to the sensuous. And what else was there? Brotherhood? Some people said that was only the consolation of moralists in old age; Mantell's monkeys knew nothing of it, for they saw at a glance the difference between red and blue.

In his abstraction his eyes encountered those of a Scandinavian girl at a neighbouring table. She bent her head modestly. That girl was instinctively right. She knew that Mantell was a very proper object for her approval. She was bowed as frail but as tenacious of life as a tinctured anemone in April. She was inextinguishable. She was a hint of the levity of beauty, which is rooted in the everlasting rocks. He did not see, nevertheless, that while admiring the flourish of Mantell's head, and his lively and bantering eyes, she had been surprised by the rapt expression of the grey-haired man who was wool-gathering beside Mantell. She wondered who he was, singular as he appeared among the other men; she was attracted by the novelty of a severity which was strangely benign, and perhaps was a little fanatical.

Then Travers forgot her, even while she was venturing another peep at him. These folk, he supposed, were like their nations; they had only just tumbled out of the cradle. Was there a word, one they would know, which would check the delightful uproar on the nursery floors? They might pause, if they heard it. They might stare; yes, and then they would laugh.

They would turn to their toys again; not ready for it yet. Whatever gracious word it was, it could not sound imperative in that noise. Thor was the chap for them, with his thundering hammer on metal. They enjoyed that. And might always enjoy it most, because time is nothing, so creation can never end. The nursery and its toys for ever! That word, if it ever came, would have to be the challenge of a trumpet. Judgment Day, children! All is over! Out goes the light; we've had enough of your little game!

Yet the right intimation might exist then, even in that room, the hint that could save; for beauty was there, though as delicate and retired as a windflower. The Graces lived, and if once known they might at least make the Yahoos less sure of the propriety of their dirt.

Not much chance of it? It was a hard lesson. Too soon yet, perhaps. Beauty was not so easily recognized, except at its origin. There it was seen and accepted without demur. Young men and maidens knew what had to be done for the good of the race without being told. The sprout of beauty was genital, and for most people it kept to its source. They were right, as far as they went. Its original purpose must be served. The first couple had eaten of the fruit of the tree of knowledge, and their children must get on with the job.

That meant evil, though, as well as good. And which grew faster? His own art showed which. It was no better than the serving of desire, the housing and decoration of money. There must come an end to that. He would let it go. Evil was getting all the help it needed. Art might have been no more, when it began, than the impulse to generation deflected from its first purpose; but then, what was lovely and of good report began with a she-wolf guarding her cubs. There are many worlds. When you see clearly which one you are in, then the time has come to depart from it.

Whatever the better word might be, it didn't mean another new London building, enormous and damned. That was not bringing design to the wilderness. That was adding to the noise and lumber. Men were entangled enough with their costly and elaborate contrivances; they had made an ugly prison for themselves, and locked it from the inside. What did they proudly call their muck, brought about by their ingenuity? Civilization. Away with it! They were fouling their star.

That was Mantell speaking to him. "What did you say?"

"I asked, where have you been the last ten minutes? You haven't answered a word I've said."

Travers mumbled. He laid his hands on the arms of his seat to raise himself, and they shook, as the ship heaved slightly. He heard the undertone of the power which was hurrying them through the night. He was turning to Mantell when he noticed a member of the orchestra bending over a fiddle, scraping and grinning. He knew that mop of hair. That was the Cockney steward; bending low over his fiddle, and grinning.

Mantell was about to speak playfully again to his companion, who was then regarding him. Mantell checked himself. That face surprised him. The man beside him looked funny. Was he sick?

"Don't let us talk, Mantell. Don't say anything. Talk only confuses."

The young man frowned in perplexity. He suspected something was a little out. There hadn't been enough wine for this. Travers didn't seem quite the thing, not quite all there.

Chapter Four

MRS. TRAVERS, AT THE OFFICE COUNTER OF THE LIVER-
pool Hotel, showed signs of haste and impatience. She
failed to disturb the averted deliberation of the clerk,
but at length he admitted that the *Cambodia* would not
be alongside the landing stage before midday. Mrs.
Travers was set at ease. She remarked apologetically
that she had been afraid she was late. The clerk was
not really busy, so he then noted his guest, because of
her voice.

"No, madam. As a rule, an incoming ship arrives
some time after the people who are anxious to meet
her."

His manner now allowed Mrs. Travers to conjecture that this slight attention to her was different from
his ordinary duties. She was a woman, that experienced
hotel clerk recognized, whose sudden appearance
proved that pleasant surprises were still possible, in
however tedious a recess in life.

Midday! Then there was plenty of time. She had

leisure in a city that was new to her. It was a day, too, which brightened the novelty. She enjoyed the challenge of strange places and new people. Out she went to meet the ship which was bringing John home. Liverpool was raw morning and uproar as she passed out of the shadow of the muffled hotel. It pleased her, that clamour and drive of a maritime city. The continuous shattering rumble of the traffic showed with what elemental energy thumped its impersonal heart. What was it John said in one of his letters? He wanted to get home to a quiet life. She was amused. That was so like him. Here was home. Didn't he know it? She enjoyed this hearty noise. It was so cheerful and thoughtless. The city trembled in its exuberance.

Did she enjoy it because his ship would soon be in? She did; but that was not the only reason. It was a blue and white day, and the tumult of a strange city's generic activity was inspiriting. It set up vibrations. It was sensational. The young world was vastly manifested, full of chances. Nothing was ever heard in John's old study; or only another match being struck; not even a merry moment whistled a tune there. She paused by an attractive shop, and there was held by a new note in the racket of the city. She forgot the window. What was that sound? It came again. A ship—

that was a ship! It was speaking. And with what a
grave voice! These shop fronts hid the sea. She knew
all the wonder of music was in that call from the unseen.

Mrs. Travers continued her leisurely walk in the direction from which the ship had called. That might
have been the *Cambodia* coming in. In what was evidently a weary moment in New York, when commer-
cial architecture had turned to dust and mortgages,
John had calmly mentioned escape from it all, a desire
for retirement. John had had enough of it. What, of
this? Did that ship's voice agree with the idea of retirement, of peaceful rest? Not a bit of it. It called the
other way. There could be no rest in the heart, when
only the voice of a ship could stir it so easily. But what
John thought was good was what other people ought
to think was good, if they were reasonable. Perhaps
he was right. He was often right, when afterwards
you thought it over in submission; though puzzling at
first. It was easy for him to be right, and difficult. He
was patient and tolerant. He could always maintain his
silence, when other people were gaily persuaded, and
wait for second thoughts. It was rather strange that
second thoughts should be best, when usually they put
a stop to pleasant things, and made one sigh. What if

we all paused for second thoughts to come along, like the police? Should we ever do anything?

No. Never do anything but look like a holy plaster Madonna on a sacred shelf who had done only one thing and thought that was enough for a lifetime. And she herself hadn't done so much as that, and it began to look as though she never would.

Here, what sort of a thought was that? That was getting near to treason—here, quick, find a second thought immediately! Well, John was a wise and squeezable companion, yet somehow a peaceful man was enough to make one break the peace. Never mind that now. He was nearly home. Besides, he had seemed despondent. America had not been what he expected. He wanted to see her instead of America. Come unto me, ye weary! Poor fellow, his heart was always being gnawed by silence. He was too sensitive, and absurdly moral. His feet were on this earth, so his spirit was in prison. O Paradise, O Paradise! But oh damn, too, for who wants rest when the band is playing? Who wants Paradise on a fine day? Why not enjoy what we've got, now we're here? It was perfectly wasteful to let the real things go, as if they weren't there for us. To stand pensively eyeing the stars! Now, how long must one wait on the stars be-

fore there is a helpful answer? They had no dealings
with us. And, if they had, they didn't seem too jolly—
catch her trying to warm her hands at the Great Bear!

She supposed she must be getting near the landing-
stage, for frequently at the end of a vista she saw the
incongruous splash of blue or red of a steamer's funnel topping the dun brickwork. Yet where was the
river? How did ships get in among the chimney pots?
She had imagined it would be easy to come upon so
big an element as the Mersey, from her hotel; but she
had never before experienced the maze with which
the contingencies of a seaport invests its ships, for the
bewilderment of all but the elect. Railway tracks and
warehouses were athwart the right direction, and dock
basins, and sheds with their doors open but leading
only to hollow gloom. No thorofare existed, apparently. She was headed off. Twenty to twelve! The
structures about her were all largely devoted to maritime affairs, but they secluded the sea; they hid their
secret from curious and ignorant eyes.

She hailed a taxicab, to the astonishment of its
driver, who made a detour, for he did not want the
journey to seem comically short. He kept to himself
the fact that the *Cambodia* was not yet alongside, and
there was no hurry; and within a reasonable circuit

brought her to an almost empty expansion of the day. There was the Mersey, conjured up by an unobserved trick.

But there was no *Cambodia*. If that liner were this side of the horizon, it was lost with other distant ships in the depth of an infinity of wind and light. If the man who was to meet her came out of that confusion of water and gleaming cloud, then Mrs. Travers told herself she could believe in miracles. Two domineering steamers were near; but the other ships were far away, were no more than the membranes of flies caught in transcendental gossamer; they did not change position or magnitude, as she peered at each hopefully. If it hadn't been for the little tugs fussing on the river disrespectfully she would have suspected that those remote ships seaward were set for ever in the dreamy immensity of space. Somebody spoke casually; "There she is."

Deep in the luminous distance was another filmy wedge, greater than the rest; its outline and colours sharpened and brightened while Mrs. Travers watched, though she could not believe it was moving. It simply enlarged with her hope.

When the liner was near she began to scrutinize acutely the thin streak of pale pink, which must have been faces, for occasionally a section moved, set above the bulwark of a lofty deck. There was hardly a feature in the pink. Everybody was the same tint. Only nameless flesh was there. Misgiving seized her. To expect to discover John in so complicated a monster was the same as expecting empty space to give up a particular ship at a fixed hour. Here was the ship, but where was her man? She was anxious. There were only people in the abstract . . . was that he? No, not John. It was a figure signalling to some one behind her.

No it was not. She saw him. She waved a hand vigorously in explosive relief. What luck! The bright void had given her what she had come for. Her weak faith in the probability of celestial law and order was uplifted, during the short while it took the ship to moor. Yet with that verification, with that fulfilment of her expectation, her little adventure began to lose its zest; in the knowledge that now they must meet she descended to the customary level of the daily hours, which are slow. She retired, in fact, now calm, to await her husband in the hall where a spate of baggage was already separating accurately to various destinies under the letters of the alphabet. She rebuked her silly head, as she watched, for supposing for one fearful moment that the large reckonings of her fellow creatures, vague and without warrant though they appeared to an innocent, could fail to shape and materialize in their due order, and at the appointed hour become satisfactory on the flat commonplace of the day's work; and tomorrow be with the old newspapers.

She hunted along the ranging letters of the alphabet, and waited under T for her husband. A trunk of his had arrived before her. What a careful world it was. It thought of everything. It knew all about idiots, and did what was necessary to keep them from wandering loose. These arrangements worked like a noiseless machine, which predestinated events. Mr. and Mrs. Travers desired to meet each other, and so her train and his ship headed directly for the letter T; and there she was.

And there was he. John detached himself from a descending stream of passengers scattering over the floor, paused, and saw his own place in a glance. He seemed tired. Why, his greeting was absolutely convincing; she went happily sparkling within before he released her. Now she knew he was glad she had come. She raised her head to meet his solemn content with the frivolity of intimacy, but was embarrassed when

38

she noticed one of the busy crowd was standing close. She had forgotten the presence of the nobodies. Who was this young man; had he a right to be shy and amused?

"Fanny, here's a shipmate of mine, Mr. Mantell."

A showy boy, not even old enough to control his start when he heard she was not John's daughter. That natural sense of possession of the young uns! They always know their downy rosiness is a woman's precious own. She took John's arm, while talking.

Yet young Mantell was never likely to be of an age when he could be unimpressed by that coolness of intelligent maturity in a slight figure that was still buoyant, as of the morning, and whose very address had the innocent candour of early light. Mrs. Travers had also the enticement of oddity in her dusky pallor, with eyes set so musingly wide apart that they roused a suspicion that she was giving more indulgent attention to your reservations than to the words you were using. Mr. Mantell felt his superior height a little less under her cool scrutiny. He suspected a likelihood that the faint lines at the corners of her mouth were of a sly humour not so very girlish. The bold curves of her nostrils hinted a delicacy that might feel disdain, without confessing it, for many things a careless man

would blunder over for their excellence. His respect
for her husband deepened. It was strange that Travers
had never mentioned her.

An Officer of the Customs brusquely intervened.
That interlude was ended. Mantell, glad to be of
service to so notable a pair, helped in the dispatch of
their cab. They departed for Lime Street Station.

Chapter Five

At the station they discovered they were mistaken about the train. That was her fault. It is so difficult to be both happy and prudent. It was not much of a mistake—only a trifle more than an hour to wait. But an hour is immense if you want to keep it. It is a considerable fragment of life if you must throw it away. Every minute of an hour to be at a standstill in that dingy vault, with nothing to happen except clouds of steam bulging at the far end of its noisy half-light! It jolted the holiday seriously, when the first excitement was over, and you wanted nothing to interrupt the excursion.

She grimaced her annoyance to John, and made a mock apology. The difficulties had begun; now he could be sure he was home. She had spoiled the celebration at the very beginning. But he appeared not to hear her. He didn't care, of course. One train was exactly like another to him. Time is only the clock, so why look at it?

What was there to do? There was the cathedral. Should they drive out to see that? No; better not to mention it. If they went there they'd lose all the trains there were. Cathedrals were not his caper, so he respected them the more, and stayed longer. No sacred vaulting, if you please. Why should they not just pose on the spot as immortals who could make all the time they required—why not loftily overlook these thousands of poor sinners hurrying because they had squandered every minute but their last, but could just about reach eternal rest with that, if they were quick? There is a lot to be said for a busy railway station; as fun, it is livelier than an empty though sacred nave.

She tried to beguile John's attention with this incident and that. She made romantic interpretations of the characters and meetings in the medley. But he was silent; he seemed to relish the novelties, yet admitted them with but a smile. Surely he must be very thankful. Whenever he was thankful he had nothing to say. Men are eloquent only when they are upset. When they are contented they brood.

A dog paused by them, tentatively. She stooped to speak to it. The dog was grateful. It never expected to be welcomed. She knew it was a male dog because its shaggy eyebrows and face were full of sad deep thought and woeful understanding. Its eyes expressed the sorrow of the stranger, far from the Argive land. She laughed, and pulled its lank ears. Its mother must have been a true terrier, but its father, the wretch, was a hound who had escaped for one night only from a black dream. Look at what he did! She turned to encourage John to lightness of heart with this lovable error, but he had gone.

Nervously she surveyed the confusion about her. It was instantly alien and uncongenial. Ah, there he came, with some newspapers. It gave her a little shock, to find nothing where he had been standing, a minute before. She hated magic and mysticism. No illusions, if you don't mind. For John did sometimes raise a doubt with a suggestion of moonshine. You looked at him, when an idea had caught him, and felt somehow you would have to keep your eyes on that man; not turn away and forget him.

The minute hand of the big station clock crawled on slowly. There was nothing of the jaunty little wrist-watch about the movement of that clock. Whenever you looked at it, it was about the same as before. It was not for man, but for all time. Mrs. Travers yawned, and idly scanned the headlines in the newspapers. Our Lucky Prince: Holes out in One.

Shock for Gardener: Baby Thown from Aeroplane.
The Crisis: Prime Minister Pleads for Faith: "England's Future to Come." Another Bank Smash: Mil-
lions Ruined: Chairman Saved by Police. All the Win-
ners. Air Record Gone: Girl Flies to Jericho: Says
She Made Bet with Mother.

That bank smash! Here was another sad accident to
the cash. The great financiers were making a habit of
crashing; perhaps their chairs were tired of stateliness
on three legs. She rustled the paper as a question at
John; did this bank business mean anything to them?
—but he had gone again. That was all right. She remembered. He said he was going to get a book. Won't
be long, dear. Where was that queer bit about a baby
and an aeroplane? Jericho? That wasn't the place. But
she must have seen it somewhere. Cricket scores. Poly-
gon Theatre. See Pearl Clotho in Love while Waiting.
All Talking.

Mrs. Travers, her attention wandering over these
tokens of unrest, forgot her surroundings. She was
only conscious that, just beyond the margins of her
opened sheet, swift shadows shuffled their feet in an
incessant pour. Was that John who had just stopped?
Only a man lighting his pipe. Give him a chance.
Broken words floated by. "Where's that little bitch?"

At an inquest held yesterday at Ancoats. . . . Pyjama Dance Tonight. "For God's sake don't hold that parcel by the string."

Here, this wouldn't do. She folded the paper, and looked round. The scene clamoured vacuously again. She suspected too much of an hour had slipped away through not watching it. What time was it now? An intermittent electric sign blinked above: Eat Mort's Sausages. Its bland irrelevance startled her. And there was the notice-board for their train; it was in.

They ought to be moving. Could he be still at the bookstall? Was it safe to leave the luggage and run over to look for him? Why didn't this everlasting stream of people stop? Damn! you couldn't see anybody in it. She risked it. She darted here and there, to corners where the traffic might be hiding him. She returned reluctantly to the luggage, which was desolate, for she was alone with it.

What could she do? There it went—the warning for their train. Too late now. The activities about her became brutal in their inattention to her alarm. A man stumbled over a corner of one of her trunks; he paused for an instant to scowl back at its owner. She stared him out. Serve him right. He ought to have broken

45

his neck. Her hands were hot. She split a glove when tugging it off.

"What, not gone yet?"

Mrs. Travers knew that voice. Some of her composure was restored by the faint resentment it aroused.

"Appearances are against me, Mr. Mantell. I won't pretend I've gone. In fact, I don't know where my husband is."

Chapter Six

WHEN TRAVERS WENT OVER TO IDLE BY THE BOOK-
stall he did not, though he was patient, find what he
wanted, because he did not know what he wanted there
till he saw it, and he did not see it. His inspection roved
without arrest over strange names and empty words.
That attraction of railway literature, like coloured
treasure displayed in a resplendent cavern set in sub-
marine twilight, naturally drew him, yet as he hovered about it he began to understand that he was a
stray from an unappreciative variety of the swarms.
The bright attraction was nothing to him; it was part
of the vagary. Other travellers, abrupt and energetic,
bustled to the light; they were sure that what they
wanted was there, asked for it curtly, and it was flung
at them. They elbowed him in his reverie.

He thought he knew of a bookshop outside the station, quite near. He remembered seeing it from the
cab. That would not take long. He strolled out into
St. George's Square. The city did not impress him as
it had his wife earlier in the day.

47

The noise of it did not quicken him. It was remote. The rumour of its energies was usual, and so it did not, as would the strangeness of a foreign note, besiege him to account for its menace. The activities around were those of the familiar shadow-show without a story, and without an end. He heard when he listened, but he was not listening, though sometimes one of its shadows became personal when it jostled him, and his attention was wakened.

He happened into a side street. Liverpool remained a blurred perception, to be brought to the foreground and within reason only by the stroke of chance. From out of its random movements a boy on a bicycle pedalled into Travers' view, whistling. The boy wabbled on a tram-track, and a huddle of rags flung itself before a motor-bus. Travers stopped. The flowing bus was immediate and enormous to flatten the rags, while the bicycle was convulsive for an instant and then lay dead in the road, which was wet. The bus wheels failed at the heap; they refused the sacrifice. They stood over it.

The heap of rags resurrected in alacrity before the bus, and was a boy again, standing with a streak of blood on his face; and the man who wanted a book became aware, in a moment, that he himself had only just

begun to breathe. The rumouring vision about him had
turned solid in a shout, and he heard his own inspiration after revival in the midst of reality. He was there.
The city had ceased to be a vagary. It was on foot, and
moving with him. The boy, smearing blood over
his face, and then inspecting his hand, began to speak
to the bus driver, and Travers, in solicitude, crossed
the road to them. The driver was pale, and was in
friendly converse with the muddy figure.

"Not hurt sonny, sure?"

"Nothing. I'm awright."

"That's nothing, that's only a scratch. You scared
me stiff. It's a lucky thing. . ."

The boy smiled shyly, and in evident surprise that
he was all right, rubbed his head.

In his relief, Travers relished this human group. To
be whirled out of nowhere among a city's flying wheels
and then into calm again made him appreciative of
existence. A stout-hearted cherub, that boy; he had
kept his colour. The driver, though, was scared. "Got
kids of my own," he muttered to Travers. All was
well. The affair was composed. No harm had been
done. The driver had shown skill on demand, and the
boy pluck. Now everybody could go on in peace as
before.

But everybody was not going on quite as before. A curious crowd was gathering about them. When Travers would have retired he discovered that he was accompanied in his interest. He could not easily depart. An eager press was hedging him in. He was the centre of an insistent and prying enquiry, which concentrated and eddied about till he lost sight of the principals in the drama. That was changing its nature, and was taking hardly more time to do it than it took a boy to get under the wheels of a bus and up again.

Was that the same bus moving off, or had another come up? As well as he could see, as he was not near enough, a horse and cart now stood on the site of the incident. Travers was nudged in confidential enquiry by a haggard man in an old cap. "What's up?"

He began to wonder whether he knew what was up or down. This might be another street rumpus. He only supposed he had known a little while ago. "A motor-bus, a boy down—nobody hurt."

The man did not listen; he showed no faith in Travers, but went on for the truth. An unlifted voice became distinct, expressing faith enough. "The bloody things didn't ought to be allowed. Nobody's safe these days."

It was answered by a bulky figure beside Travers. "What do you know about it? I saw it. Be fair. The motor-bike was on its proper side."

"But," corrected Travers gently, "the boy's was only an ordinary bicycle."

The man bent down on him a long and dirty look. "Who pulled your chain? Call me a liar?"

"Not at all. You may be, but that's not my business."

Travers met a measuring glare from his challenger in grace, and gave him an affable nod. The man was puzzled. Travers was not large, nor angry, and not a boss, nor an easy clerk who was asking for it like a fool; the stranger withdrew his threat; he left this curiosity alone.

Travers, though noting it so closely, did not falter before the unpropitious aspect of this fellow. It heartened him. Another object on two legs was nothing to worry about; he never related it to the impersonal movements of the multitude, which he feared. To him those movements were incredible. They were no more sensible to persuasion than the hot bowels of Etna, which are immortal in the body of earth, and pour flames over vineyards when their mysterious balance is upset. He shrank from the unrest of mankind, for that comes of nobody knows what conjunction of blind powers engendering. But a fellow creature was only like himself, a fugitive from Eden, unable to find his way back, and subject to irritation; he was easy to face. Travers was not indignant with this stranger, but only regretful that the simple truth should be assailed, when it was known.

He made no further effort to escape. Another interest held him. As he knew what had caused this crowd, and its mistakes, he could not leave it. He listened, and with increasing surprise, to the sound of the people. The murmuring of the crowd was like that of an incoming tide, or like a wind rising in the ancient woods, stirring forgotten things, muttering in the heart of the woods; it might rise to anything. It was an elemental sound. It was disquieting to listen to the muttering in the dim heart of these woods.

And when he heard words clearly they had gone far from the cause which had assembled the people. How far would they go? Yet he knew, for he could hear the very accent, that everybody there was eager to straighten a matter in the name of justice. There were convincing words sent across the throng in scorn of foul play, or in sympathy with virtue. Travers was aware of a mystery. He discovered that though his fellow creatures were convinced of the truth of a matter of which they knew nothing but rumours misbe-

gotten, yet they were loyal souls who loved fair deal-
ing. A storm could rise among honest and loyal hearts
for a reason in the void. The people around him were
not deluded. They knew they were not, for their
minds were set in rectitude, so they could not be
wrong.

"The poor kid."

"It's a shame. Where's the ambulance?"

" 'E'll be dead before they get 'ere."

They wanted to see the victim. They wanted to see
why they were there. It was necessary to blame something. Travers was pushed about, for he had little will
of his own. He stepped out because he had to go, and
he grew hot. A common cause had stirred these many
expectant hearts, if they did not rightly know what
it was; though that was of less importance, for they
were stirred, and pulses are seldom favoured with an
excuse for a faster beat now the drill of cities has reduced our green playground to the flat gravel of a
barrack square.

"It's the second this week in this street."

"What? I say it was. You weren't here."

"I wasn't? I know what you are. You're another
record-smasher, and what's more, that face of yourn
'u'd smash all records quicker than yer ruddy bike."

Sides were being formed, by those lucky enough to share the common interest in a dramatic event they had not witnessed. The uncertainty in the gathering only served to increase the confidence of the seekers after justice, for doubts are unnecessary when reason is absent.

" 'Aven't 'orses got as much right as motors?"

" 'Orses? What about us? Can't we walk the streets without a licence?"

"You've got it. We're only jay walkers."

At least Travers could hear that the people about him were humane and generous. Instinct is all we need to tell us that right must be supported, or peace and civility will cease. The desire for swift justice grew in warmth.

"There ought to be a law against it."

"Law! What for? It's only us."

Travers was not unaffected by the uprising of the liberal spirit of the folk. His contact with the crowd was close, and he received something from it. The general umbilical tie was thrilled, and he with the rest felt the pulse of his origin. For his part, he was moved to see the need for intercession. He knew from what cause these contentious noises had arisen; and if a man would cool the factions and restore harmony, he must

54

let the truth be known. The truth is simple, as are the warm hearts of our fellow men; but the truth was getting mixed by the variousness of the hearts.

There was a heated and continuous dispute beside him. It concerned the greater mobility and usefulness of motor-buses, and the antiquity and public danger of tram-lines. It did not permit of question and answer, because there came no pause in the flow of words. It was a dual commination, nose to nose. Travers could hear that both men were wrong, and he supposed that appeasement must come if they learned they had nothing to quarrel about, because the event itself was different, and was past. He attempted it. He laid a friendly hand on the arm of one of the disputants, and he was successful. The quarrel was hushed. This one of the pair regarded Travers as though he were trying to believe him, yet found it hard.

" 'Ear 'im?" he asked of the other, when he had recovered from his wonder. " 'Ear this bird? Look, 'ere's Jesus lost 'is whiskers."

The other man did not smile. Apparently he was not interested in Travers, for he was looking elsewhere in contemplative indifference. Yet suddenly he seemed to remember that in an unhelpful interval he was losing his enjoyment, and he swerved to bend over the interruption. His face was disparaging.

"Keep your door shut," he ordered Travers. "Who asked you to chip in? Your car barge into the tram? That how you know?"

Travers recovered from his recoil, and met his adversary with a glance of stern reproof; but that was only to hide his disenchantment. The hostility of the face which waited for his answer agitated him. It was bleak and beyond appeal. It craned as inhuman as one of Hydra's many heads. It roused his abhorrence of violence and ugliness. His car and a tram! It was perverse and malignant. Here were men, making trouble when there was enough of it. What does one do with ignorance when it is everywhere and vicious? Then, in relief, he saw a helmet of the law making through the scattering mob with speed, but in that instant his hat abruptly flew off, and he dropped. A welter of quick legs wavered about him, and the nails of a boot vehemently bit into his hand.

A policeman hauled him up. "What's all this about? You ought to know better than this."

Chapter Seven

TRAVERS TRIED TO STEADY HIMSELF TO A COURTEOUS poise. The daft antics of men whirled about in a haze of demented speed; or stood still unexpectedly for a moment, waiting to be explained, like this. He gave the policeman infirm but respectful attention. The law and its questions was the present countenance to reality, and he did his best to fix its rightful place in recent events, but he could not succeed on the instant. He began to suspect, while the policeman waited for an answer, that somehow he was at fault. The street had fallen strangely quiet, except for a humming, which was in his head.

The sergeant spoke again, but to some one behind him. "Here, come here, you."

Somebody came, and stood beside Travers. The policeman's voice was blunt.

"What's the game? Didn't I see you hit a man?"

"You did that, sergeant, and I think he got it where he didn't want it. He went for this gentleman, but I put him off his stroke."

"What's it all about?"

"Search me for it. I wasn't here at the start, worse luck, but it had the makings of a tidy fuss when you came up."

The policeman pointed his thumb at Travers. "What was he doing?"

"Well, I should say he was just standing still because he couldn't move on. He was as quiet as a sergeant off duty."

"Was he, though. Sure you don't know him?"

"As sure as I know you, Sergeant Brennan."

"Then you know enough to mind your eye when you see me. Be off with you."

Travers began to revive, and to see it all a little more clearly. He fancied he could show the absurdity of this, and began to speak, but the policeman made a negative and good-natured gesture. "Sure it's all right." He smiled condolingly. "I wouldn't have said you were scrapping, mister. I can't see you doing it. Take a bit of advice. When you see trouble in the town, go for a sharp five minutes' walk, and don't look back."

Travers was grateful; he detached himself, and drifted away. The man who knew the sergeant went with him, and this stranger, after a suitable interval, spoke low through a twisted mouth. "Smart man, the sergeant, and if he was as smart as he fancies he is he'd know more than he does. . . . Far to go?"

"No. Only to the station."

"Lime Street? If you are not in a hurry for a train, drop into my place. You'll have to pass it. You want some tidying up."

Travers walked on, and considered this. He paused, and took out his watch, and considered that, without noting what hour it gave, nor the fact that it had stopped. Vaguely he returned the watch. It was a habit of his to take out his watch and consider its face without reading it, for so he found the time he wanted, a space in which he could determine that a problem had to be settled. He regarded the stranger doubtfully, and then walked on with him, more or less in the hour of his false time-keeper. He kept pace along the street with his new companion, talking in a desultory way.

Somehow, he surmised that he was not going in the right direction, and not with the right party. He wished he knew the right way; but it is something when at last you have no doubt the old way leads only to damnation. That was settled. Damnation is deserved when you see it ahead and work for it. The change had come, and Fanny would have to know what it was.

But what was it? How to persuade a good and reasonable creature, when your conviction is as unreasonable as a spring morning? People do not trust new light. It is not as comforting as old dusk in which you can't see that things are wrong. But he would add not another infernal stone to the celebration of money. It had enough. Not another touch of ugliness to the world, if he could dodge it.

Could he dodge it? He was fairly caught in an ugly mess ten minutes ago. Men grow to be like the things which duty tells them they must do. When they build their dark satanic mills then the suggestion of a possible Jerusalem is the threat of an enemy. Enemies should die, and so they know they are righteous when they continue to defile England's green and pleasant land. They are not indifferent to beauty; they hate it, for it opposes their necessity. It is in their way. And they grow to be like the things they do. Their heads become as clever and efficient as little power-stations. And they are all alike; only some move faster than others; some have more efficient boxes of brains. This fellow with him worked on a slick gearing. His head was a box of clever tricks. So many people were like

it; their instrumental brains were prompted auto-
matically, and that raised the ugly fuss, for their bellies were full of the explosive instincts of savages.
Fanny was never wrong except when she was clever,
and all her cleverness would come out now, to keep
things as they were. Every woman knows it is
safer to do that. To keep things as they are! But those
things are dead, or ought to be. It is the real folly to
look for life in that sepulchre.

Still, it was Fanny who had done most to give him
different eyes. When he thought of her, she was a
token of the secret and enduring values. But how
she would laugh at that! And she would be right.
Women don't want to be tokens of rare notions, but
wives and mothers.

Travers turned abruptly to a question. "What did
you say? Yes, New York. Yes. I've just got back."

"How are things there now?"

"Why, how are they here? There's nothing but the
sea between us."

The stranger glanced sharply at Travers, who was
unaware of it, and walked on in meditation. To know
Fanny was like assurance of God, though the sky
fell, being nothing. He had the memory of her whenever he was bent under the weight of time and the

black omen of futility. She was amaranthine, like Aphrodite. The sight of her that morning was as good as that sunrise long ago at Taormina. It was dark in a strange room, and he opened the shutters and stepped out. The truth had dawned, and there he was. It made him young and stark in an uprising of light. No more age and disbelief. The gods had come. Eos was born, flame-haired and lovely. The sea had the colours of a dove's throat, and the sky was celebrating. Fanny was the same as that dilation of glory over the world. She wasn't reason, but she was meaning, though it was hard to say what the meaning was, except that it was good. She was perpetual life. She never knew that his best work had flowed—just when it was jammed, too—because she had come in with a laugh, and was nonsensical. The right things were born when she laughed. She was a good mother, but didn't know it, and regretted that she was not. Her very fun could convince him; that was release enough. For it is right in the gods to smile at us in amusement, and give us faith. Faith is knowledge transcended. You can't go back to concrete and steel after Eos has been conjured up. Then the old game is dead. It is dead.

The stranger beside him stopped, by the shop window of a florist and seedsman, and Travers saw at once it was a likely place for a halt. The window displayed roses chiefly; it had a gallery of chosen blooms, each with a name. The roses were posed singly, in sprays, as though they were exclusive and patrician. They accorded with his reverie. He turned to the stranger to show his approval, and suggested that there was no word for that display, but the stranger waved a hand to the name-board over the shop. "That's me," he said. Travers read it. P. Quirke.

"You are Mr. Quirke?"

The florist nodded his head sadly, in waggish acknowledgment.

Quirke! It was not a joyous name. It was not so good as the name of his roses, not like Rayon d'Or, or Euphrosyne. Quirke! It might indicate derisive reservations, it might hint mockery, it was not a happy admission.

"What roses you've got, Mr. Quirke," said Travers, going close to the window. "I've never seen any so good—but I know nothing about them, except that they are roses. My place is in London, the middle of it, and nothing grows there but moss." He smiled at an idea. "Tell me, is this your notion of publishing what is acceptable and of good report?"

"Publishing which?" asked Mr. Quirke.

"Well, some people think we should all die if we didn't get news of this sort. You've made a sound contribution."

"All right," muttered Mr. Quirke, "those roses are as cheap as you'd find anywhere."

Travers wondered whether he was mistaken in this man. He had had a suspicion of Quirke. There was something queer about him, perhaps sinister. Anyhow, he seemed to have found names for these roses, these variations of joy. Triomphe Orleanais—Irish Fireflame —Snow Queen. Did Quirke read Hans Andersen? Château de Clos Voquet. And had he chosen dinners in Burgundy? Ariel—High Dawn—Susan Dickinson. Was that one named after a golden lady he knew? Then it would be beneficial to meet her.

Quirke showed a little impatience. "Come inside," he said.

Travers took another look at his watch, saw no difference betokened there, and entered. He inhaled the smell of that shop. It was not rich, but earthy and candid, with only a trace of sweetness. That smell must come, thought he, from the very roots. One of the walls was a height of small mahogany boxes, apparently laden with seeds, and it pleased the visitor to reflect that this catacomb of dry dust was dynamic.

It could break the crust of winter, if used. Trusses of bass were suspended from hooks. A board was cross-hatched with bands of elastic, which were loaded with small envelopes, each packet gay and different with the portrait of a flower. He followed Quirke along a counter which was wet through the watering of loose heaps of flowers and leaves, and several girls stood there deftly weaving them into crosses and wreaths. Travers noticed a closer application to the task when Mr. Quirke paused to make a polite enquiry to one of his assistants.

"That cross gone to the Murpheys?"

"Not yet, sir."

"Are we going to miss another funeral?"

"No, sir."

"There's one we won't miss if we do." He pushed through a door into a room beyond, and Travers followed.

Chapter Eight

MRS. TRAVERS FELT THAT HER MIND HAD SUNK INTO the middle of herself, tiny and still. It had been on the surface, scattered and distracted. It had retired for safety to a central quiet. It watched from within. Young Mantell couldn't hear it, when she had to answer him. He was talking then. He had another suggestion to make. They had followed his hopeful suggestions till now she was an atheist. She could believe in nothing whatever. Mantell was a good fellow to give his time like this. He had thought since yesterday of more ways of finding John than she would have seen, even if she had been sensible; but they were all empty. Incredible! You could fall into a city, as into the sea, and leave no mark. A wind had passed, and had blown John out. Could he be given a shape again?

Mantell had been telling her about a last dinner with John in the ship. What did he mean? Did he want to hint, but was too polite to say it, that John had gone potty? Much he knew of him! John was sane enough, but he had unexpected ways. He would never lose himself; not like that. But they could lose him. She ought not to have lost sight of him.

Now Mantell had another idea. He thought there might be a chance; he dived into a telephone box. If it wasn't the last chance it was the last but one. Mrs. Travers watched him within the glass box. She could see his jaw working, but could hear nothing. The reflections in the glass made the man within as evasive as the man they sought. Two steps this way, and Mantell had vanished from the box without coming out. She had to move her head to put him back into it. His jaw was still working, but she could see by his attitude that he might as well drop it. There was no sound, and nothing but reflections on the surface, which changed when you moved.

Mantell came out. He did not speak to her, and she understood there was no question worth the asking. This was a street she had seen before. She passed through it on the way to the ship. She remembered it— there across the way was that florist's. The extraordinary roses were still in the window, but they were as confusing as the reflections in the glass. Just move your head a bit, and you change the look of things. Even beauty could be awful in its complete indifference to pain. That might mean pain was of no importance; yet one felt it. Could even roses be ironic?

It was a shock, the uncovering of a head that morning, in the mortuary. Mantell, good fellow, offered to go. A suicide, a man unknown. But she wasn't going to shirk it. It had to be done. Certainly it was not going to prove to be John, but as the doubt existed, she must settle it. And who was he? Was anyone seeking that awful reflection—that weary old mask looking at the ceiling, its mouth open? She hadn't wanted him, but she had found him, when looking for another man, and now her memory would have to keep him. Nothing had happened in Liverpool, the police said; only that; and a street accident but nobody hurt; and a fire in a ship's hold. They would make enquiries. Call again in the morning. Leave your hotel address.

There seemed to be nothing more they could do. They had done everything and must sit as failures, quite still. That was why Mantell annoyed her, absently performing the solemn rite of tapping his cigarette, with a wise look on his strong face, like a young elegant in a film drama kindly considering the folly of a helpless virgin. She could see herself in a mirror across the hotel lounge, and it was nice of any young man to be kind to a woman with so cheerless an eye, especially because she had only mislaid her husband. He had improved since the day she met him on the landing-stage. He was not such a boy, and he had the virtue of silence when there was nothing much to say, but he was not showing it at that moment. He couldn't get that last dinner in the ship out of his thoughts. He considered it seriously, deliberately tapping a cigarette. He seemed to think John had lost his reason. Only temporarily. Oh yes. He didn't know that John never had any reason to lose, not any worth discussing in a sociable way. What John had he never used, except mathematically—making four out of two and two. He used to say that if he waited for reason to argue an idea into being, then not a brick would ever be laid. Laying bricks was science, but it could not get going till it had the word, and the word was never reasonable, for it might be good or bad. She could not tell Mantell that. He might think she was potty, too; for he looked a sensible fellow. She could see why John was attracted to him. He was big, but lithesome in his movements. He could come out of repose, and the silly rite of tapping cigarettes, like a fine animal suddenly alert.

No, she would not stay for dinner. She would give him some time to himself. He deserved it. Mrs. Travers, in the silence of her room, alone with unresponsive hotel furniture, almost regretted that she had not stayed with Mantell. Nothing but time and space, John once told her, in one of his more confiding moments, could ever separate them. Well, what was the distance in space now? That would be worth knowing. And it would be consoling, she imagined, when pensive before the framed hotel-regulations, "Switch off the light when not in use," if time were only the same as indifference. Switch off time when not in use? There was all the time, she foresaw, between then and the next daylight; the clock would attend to that, while she waited.

She stood as though trying to divine whatever might be hidden in the grate of the fireplace, which was empty, and the recollection came of John shaking her out of sleep one night. He stood over her with a lighted candle, and when the certainty reached him that she was watching him, wide awake, she could see fear leaving his face. He said he was scared, and certainly he appeared to be. He said no more then, but slid his fingers over her brow, to verify her, and went away.

She had been curious about it next morning, but he

had tried to evade her curiosity. Had he been dreaming?

Well, yes. He had been dreaming. He smiled, but she saw he was not quite happy about it, even then. He watched her across the coffee-pot and toast and newspaper as though he might fall into the dream again, and he didn't want to be caught a second time. He said some queer things about it, later—he spoke as though once the earth had stopped spinning for him, and then had gone on, leaving him in one day, and her in another.

They had been travelling together, he told her, and had come to a strange city. They went to an old hotel, the sort of hotel John always sought. There was the usual hall of the days of the stage-coaches, its necessary doors placed where nobody would expect to find them, a glass and mahogany office, and porters with luggage. They were shown to remote upper rooms, and had ordered tea, and he had strolled out for tobacco. From the way John spoke he would have known that place again. He went along a corridor, but met nothing but aspidistras and palms and engravings after Landseer. He descended the claret-coloured carpet of a broad stairway, round and about, and nobody was there, either. John said there was a lift; but

71

catch him using a lift. You had to have contact with people in a lift. He came to another hall, with a door to a street. That street was strange. He got his tobacco, and wandered about, and then found the right street, though it seemed a little different from his recollection of it. There were signs in it he had not noticed before, and he was uncertain he had hit it until he recognized the entrance to the hotel.

The same queer old entrance; but inside he was shocked, for he did not know the place. It was all new. The porters were busy with luggage there, as before, but it was no good looking for me. He knew that. It was the same house, but in another year.

Chapter Nine

WHEN TRAVERS AND QUIRKE ENTERED THAT ROOM BE-
yond the seed-store they found two men standing at
a table on which they kept a map open by resting their
palms on it. They were surprised to see Quirke was
not alone, and apparently so was the map, for as restraint was taken from its margins it shrank into the
reticence of a roll.

Quirke half-opened it again, laid it down indif-
ferently, and presently picked it up and used it as a
pointer in conversation. He was on easy terms with
these others, and was allusive about an enterprise
which they shared with him. His behaviour reassured
them. Quirke's discerning mind told him that so innocent a fellow as Travers would learn no more from
a bare glance at a special chart than he had out of a
loud noise in the street. He had speculated on the
probability that the childlike nature of Travers, as he
seemed to be a gentleman, and was not altogether daft,
might have advantages; for it would be a pity to waste

anything that has some quality until you know it is no good to you. There was nothing to warn him that Travers, in the instant before the map closed up, recognized that coast-line as readily as he would his own features in an unexpected mirror; besides, maps were habitual fun for him. He thought it strange to see a chart of Colonna in that room, but was too polite to show his interest. He was still more interested when he heard those three unlikely men talking freely of that secluded and agreeable island, where only goats wandered about the ruins once frequented by the immortals, and the sea below was so early and vacant a blue that you couldn't be sure whether already Argo had passed the promontory, or would be abeam of it presently. Travers listened. The new felicity of that shore seemed to depend on its likelihood for a wireless station.

"I didn't expect you back so soon." The florist addressed himself to a man whose massive body and grey and craggy head could make his assumed expression of grievous resignation to a hard lot mirthful to his friends. "I've told everybody the skipper wouldn't be here for a day or two. If you're ready to push off, the men are ready to be signed on."

"They are? That's fine. When can they come out of the infirmary?"

Quirke chuckled. "They're young uns. Praise God for young uns out of work. These fellows will do anything for a change, and don't care what they get for it." He went to a cupboard and returned with a bottle and glasses. Travers noticed then that Quirke's lumpy and sallow face was memorable. It was shiny with moisture. His mouth was mobile, a long slit under restraint, and one eye had a habit of nervously twitching, when he was speaking, as if to warn you humorously that what he was saying was only spoof.

The captain was idly reminiscent. "When I was in London—Quirke, are you listening?—I said when I was in London I saw the boss for the first time. He sent for me. I couldn't find my halo, I was so surprised. He's the only owner who ever sent for me, so I knew he must want to worry something out of me not in the articles."

"Quite an honour."

"Think so? All right. Anyhow, it's fine to know a ship's owner is more real than lunars to the steward. Nowadays the boss is about the same as mumbo-jumbo. Marine superintendents and all sorts come to see me, and pretend they know God is saying so and so. They are so serious I have to believe it. But who is he? Damned if I know."

"You know now."

"Do I? I wonder. I've seen him, so I can't help wondering whether there's a lot of artful dodgery going on behind him—some gang of almighty glories without names, up to their larks, and he's the only one who ever shows himself." The seaman gazed upwards at his cigar smoke. "I used to think the boss was just a name, to keep us quiet. It was like saying Lord Snarge to yourself, for comfort; just as you say Hell when you have to do fool things because of what somebody calls instructions. See here, Quirke, you know his lordship. You knew him when you were artful kids together—a pair of beauties the police missed, I must say. Tell me, how does he do it—ships, newspapers, wireless, cinema-palaces, frozen meat, mining concessions, and oil? And women. I'd forgotten them, but they say he never does, till afterwards. How does he do it?"

"It's magic. Now you see it, and now you don't, and all that."

The captain shook his head regretfully. "I shall never see it. Look at me! I'm big enough, but one ship is all I can manage at a time, and one woman, though she doesn't believe it. There it is. I've seen this god of ours, and he's a shabby little man with a kind face like a deacon hoping you'll put a shilling in the plate, but not if you can't afford it. I wonder he didn't ask me if the baby's cough was better. Sometimes he smiles. Have you ever noticed it? His smile made me anxious about my pocket-book, but I didn't like to feel it, he seemed so kind. I could only hope I'd still got it in my pocket. Does anyone ever meet him without losing something?"

Quirke's eye twitched. "Think of the good he does."

"Not me. I can't. His smile is all I can think about. I don't enjoy it, somehow. I shouldn't like the compass to see it, unexpected."

"I wish I knew how he does it," grumbled Quirke.

"I dare say you do. You would," agreed the seaman, "though you wouldn't tell me if you knew. But give me a simple life, as it's short, and I don't know whether I'll get any more. You know, the boss seemed so gentle that I tried to get another ship for this job. The *Cairngorm* isn't a jewel. She's a bitch. Last voyage I stayed in Havre three days. I called it weather-bound, and got a cable every few hours. Did I know I was on a time-charter? Did I know it had nearly expired? Did I not! Why was I weather-bound? You'd know why, if you'd ever had a voyage in the dear old *Cairngorm*. She'd make you moor alongside a yellow-fever epidemic, for comfort, when there's weather. She's the company's ship to recommend to a board of directors for a pleasure cruise."

Quirke's mouth went sideways. "Did he give you another ship?"

The captain did not answer. He poured out more whiskey, sorrowfully. Travers laughed with the others.

"What's her speed?" asked Quirke. "How long will she take to get out?"

"Now, she's done nine when we weren't looking, but as for when we'll arrive, I don't know, and wouldn't tell you if I did. Maybe we shan't go out direct. We may get other orders. And if anything stops us from getting out you'll see it in the papers— and if we get out all right you may see it in the papers just the same, from all I hear. His lordship warned me there's a foreign bunch also after the island for a wireless station. There's been protests. Some high and noble hocus is going on. Has the boss got the rights?" The captain turned to the other man. "I didn't like to ask him. Has he wangled the ownership? You ought to know. You're one of the engineers. You won't put in your concrete without knowing it's yours?"

"Why, yes, I shall put it in. The boss knows what he is doing. If he sent me a chit to erect pylons in St. James's Park I'd begin."

"Suppose people kicked?"

The engineer was faintly superior. He readjusted his eye-glasses. "We're used to it. They always kick. We push on with the job and take no notice. The thing is to get the foundation done. Once we've got our base fixed they see it's no good kicking."

"I see."

Their comments became brief and allusive. The captain described the site to the engineer. It was level, but some rubbish would have to be cleared. The ground was littered. Old buildings were standing, and they were of solid masonry. But the engineer's interest was slight. Travers, however, showed more concern.

"What will you do with them?"

This question from a man he had forgotten was in the room quickened the engineer. "Do? My dear sir, I don't know what the buildings are, but I expect a little dynamite will help. It won't take long."

Travers glanced at the florist, who was not looking at him, but was bent over the map. "I don't see them

79

marked here," said Quirke. "There's nothing here. I thought it was open country. The buildings are not in use, are they?"

The seaman was indifferent. "In use, no. They're nothing. I've been up there. That old stoneyard wouldn't be marked. A lot of it is lying around loose. I picked up a little figure of a boy there—might have been a girl, I don't know—and brought it away as a curio. The Board of Trade man at the docks gave me a quid for it, and seemed to think he was lucky. There's one building that's pretty solid, all marble, but it won't give any trouble. Easy to shift it."

Travers felt a need to speak, but he could not ease away a congestion of words to express astonishment, alarm, protest, and disbelief, so he was fixed in silent dismay. Somehow he must be mistaken. Surely what he had heard could have no real meaning? It wouldn't give any trouble, that building, though it was all marble. It was a temple to Apollo; that they didn't know. It would be easy to shift it; of that they were sure. Steel masts would go there, instead of a sign to the leader of the muses. It was easy to destroy the peace, the aromatic herbs, and the white colonnade; they had dynamite. It wouldn't take long. For over two thousand years the god of light had kept his house for those who could face the light. The light would go out. Another need had arisen. Not here, O Apollo! Who now? Lord Snarge.

The three of them were still looking at the map, yet they saw nothing in it but Snarge, and Travers couldn't tell them what else was there. He couldn't begin to tell them. There was no approach. If he tried, the engineer would merely adjust nervously those eyeglasses under his frowning forehead and scrubbing-brush hair. What could he say? They didn't even understand his language; they might be Hottentots cleverer than himself. When Quirke turned, Travers had gone.

Chapter Ten

His departure was too much like the swift passing of a shadow to be noticed in a busy shop. As he came into the street he glanced this way and that, still in haste, but perhaps doubtful of the more direct road to Colonna. The city opposed him in indifference with the ponderous measure of its life. Its activities were huge and continuous with an alien purpose that thwarted his mood.

Across the street was a motor-garage, a deep crystal cavern where a herd of sleek monsters lay in ambush with their glossy heads to the traffic; outside it an attendant in a white robe was jerking a handle with desperate spurts in the nose of a reluctant engine, which snorted at him, but was resistant. That scene was occulted by the clanging charge of a tram. The mass and speed of the city sobered him. The draught of the tram whirled an empty paper bag to his feet. He stood and frowned at it. He saw that had as much power over the way of the wind as he himself, or a temple. Thus the wind blew. The chance eddies of the traffic of men caught up even altars, and they went with the straws.

How save a temple, which stood in the way when the flux of doctrine veered? It must go, no better than a paper bag. It was empty. There was no power to save whatever had lost its appeal to men. Even Apollo must go; his comeliness was transformed into the streamlines of a machine. So men preferred to have it. The winds of doctrine had blown it into that. The god's new temple was that house of automobiles across the street. He was there now, not in Colonna, and if you could not find him there you must do without him. The gods were protean; they had the nature we gave them; so what could abide?

He found himself in Lime Street Station again, where he peered, watchful and pensive, as if for a lost thought. A shout disordered him, Gangway Please, and he swerved from the silent glide of an electrical truck. The eddies of traffic still whirled, and he could not stand and consider where he was, and why, any more than the straws. He was trivial and overborne. He gave another look round the station, still uncertain, except of vague loss. He saw outside that night was welling in the streets. The bases of the grim buildings

83

were deeply submerged. The rising darkness was already pointed and shot with brilliant planets and meteors, but the calm sky was saffron in an afterglow, and on that the high ridges and towers of the city projected in sharp ebony.

Chapter Eleven

HE MERGED WITH THE NIGHT INTO WHICH THE CITY was foundering. He looked up once again; the sky was nearly out. He saw it as a faint memory of what would not return. Any assurance it ever had was almost gone.

And of what, he began to doubt, could it assure? This lower darkness, thought he, into which he was descending, could succeed without supernal lights. It had plenty of its own sort. A revelation from above would not show it what it wanted. It could do better without that illumination. This place lit its own lamps. They sufficed. It knew the sort of light necessary for the work it was at. When we are in the nethermost, when we have gone down out of day, and there is no shining horizon and meridian, we must trim our own glims, or go without. This place had the display it wanted. As his sky had gone, and he had no light of his own to take down with him, he must use such as he found there.

Anyhow, he was not alone. A multitude of phan-

toms accompanied him. The obscurity of the lower-
most was populous. These hurrying spectres were lost,
too, but they were of one accord about it. They were
not dismayed. They were at home in the dark, and
sometimes laughed. It was nothing to them that day
was elsewhere, and they were benighted. Here was the
only place and light they knew.

Lucky spectres! Travers supposed, as he wandered
on, that it might be better never to see light, if you
cannot use it. How fortunate were these shades about
him! Their eyes were not bewildered by a glory which
had startled them once, and vanished. They had nothing to forget. What could anyone do with the brightness of a rising that surprised the darkness of a settled
and accepted earth, and made it monstrous, yet was
immediately gone? It could not be followed. Apollo
was dead. His light was out. Its origin was unknown.
Now he could not believe he had seen it.

Fanny was right. The materialists were right. The
man who fancies he has seen such a light had better
get a grocer's candle. That lasts longer and shows
more. Yet such a man, checked by his fancy, most
likely would sooner sit in his cellar gloom and nurse
his madness. Now, wondered Travers, am I mad, or
coming to reason?

He could hear laughter among the shades. That was cheering, if a reason for it was unknown. No doubt all the best jokes sink down to Pluto; where affairs cannot grow worse there is nothing to restrain merriment. Hades has the fun, for it has nothing better. Sometimes he heard a voice, and a distinct but irrelevant word. He stopped once because he heard singing. It was above his head, in the doorway of a shop. He looked for the singer. It was a hollow voice, inhumanly magnified and indifferent, for only Travers was listening to it. But nobody was singing. It was a voice out of nowhere—out of Paris or Moscow or Philadelphia, maybe—caught on some wires the shop had set for wandering voices. It was a disembodied voice, strung in the trap of a Cimmerian waste, and howling at its capture. The shopkeeper ought to release it.

It was in keeping with a city at night, that music. It was by chance out of anywhere, addressed to nobody, and meant nothing. Travers turned away. It was the right voice for darkness. The vacant singing still blared behind him, a meaningless wonder. He supposed the voice might be chanting, to those who would not listen, the history and virtues of their city, and the eternal nature of the rock on which it stood. Its music suggested that theme. But it was an impersonal stentor and he could catch no clue. No clue existed in a metropolis of shades, a labyrinth of dazzle and murk, with its streaks and blotches of light, bodiless sounds, and abrupt starless gulfs. It had only the significance of an ocean-floor, sunk far below the penetration of the sun and the sounding of reason. It was there, and that was all. He watched, while across the depth of one dark gulf glided the glowing body of a tram. A motor-car with a glistening back and stalked and staring eyes came at him. They had their own lustre, these monsters, as though they lurked amid abysmal reefs and algæ. The nature of the rock on which the city stood? Eternal virtue was in the sea-floor, if one but knew it. It was not likely to give way. The ooze was based on the same will. Its monsters obeyed the same urge, and smaller things got out of the path.

What could change it? Was there a word to inform it, a light to civilize glistening bulks and stalked and fumbling eyes? Those questions were like stones dropped into the sea. They joined the detritus of time. The appeals of the faithful, the sacrifices of the martyrs, go to join the trilobites.

There can be no answer. The Sphinx is eyeless. It has no ears. Its flinty face has never moved. It does not know it keeps a secret, which men passionately ques-

tion. Men in Memphis had questioned it, but there in
the desert the stony face still is, though the luckless
hearts which beat against it had long mingled with the
sands; the desert had them, and their city. Other soli-
taries that night, he remembered, in London and New
York, were talking to the dark, as he was. Their own
ears knew their prayers, before dust filled them. They
wanted no more than a star-glint to see them past midnight, but Aldebaran and the rest do not shine for that.

Men will have to do without an answer. But do
what, for the desert? The desert does not know good
and evil. The saint and the usurer of Memphis were
loose and mingled together in the dunes. It comes to
that. There is no evil, when all the clocks stop, and
no good. They belong to time, and end with it. This
place in which he was lost was no better and no worse
than on the night when icebergs and glaciers slid over
its site, and men had not yet come to look to the stars
for what they would never see.

Chapter Twelve

THERE WAS THE RIVER. SUDDENLY ITS CLEAR DARKNESS was before him, deep and void as antiquity. He could hear the water, when he listened, plainer than he could see it, and its soughing carried out his interrogations to wherever the tide was going. The tide was talking to itself. He, too, had the same mark of lunacy. He and the tide knew each other. There were far gleams upon it, the signs of those who had parted from this world and were adrift beyond the verge. They had floated off before him.

Well, he could not follow at once. There was no way. Charon did not seem to be about just then—not expecting him so soon, very likely. The old boy had enough to do, and ought not to be hustled. Travers watched for a time the glints wandering in the deeps, and then turned again into the chasms between the warehouses and institutions of a city. This was his luck, as far as he had got, and he must wait.

Yet at midnight, how those looming monuments

showed for what they were, a necropolis of wrongs, of the errors of men which tombs cannot keep, of evils as old as greed and the love of power, of ancient opinions that would not bear looking at now, buried and forgotten, but potent. Those thoughts pervaded it. It was their dædalian lair. They were the stealing suggestions, haunting the souls of the quick, and waiting on the unborn to possess them. This city was in a new age, but its growing stones were rooted in the will of the dead, and enlarged it. The dead continued to govern. Why doubt immortality? There is no escape from the past, for it is present. Its pall was upon the city, like a night no morning could lift. What sun could penetrate these vaults, to sweeten the emanation from corruption which motived the nostrils of the living?

His hand rested on a wall, and the bricks were alive. Here actually it was, the spirit of the place. The wall responded to a subterranean vibration. Power was about, somewhere underground, secretly energizing the veins and conduits of the city while its people slept. This was the temple to it. The god of the commune was at home, and he was awake and enormously at work. His wheels and metallic bowels were answering the prayers of his worshippers. They had given their deity life and had set him going, and here it was, whatever it was, inevitably fulfilling their desires.

A stream of light went across the street from an opening in this wall, and there he peered into the temple to power, and heard the continuous purring of its control. He saw immense drums spinning with a mercurial velocity that feigned stillness. The monsters were crouching in pits, and had no apparent movement, yet gleams were entangled in their unseen revolutions and flickered in struggles to escape. They could not escape. The bolts of Zeus could not compete with that.

Man's speed had overtaken light. Travers' own feet trembled involuntarily where they stood, shaken by the energy of this god of man's making. An attendant was posed within, motionless before a monster, his head reverently bent to the glinting exactitude of its rhythm, as if fascinated by its shimmering celerity and confident purling. The attendant priest gently touched his charge in familiarity and watchful unconcern. He was at ease in Zion.

Travers acknowledged the beauty of that scene. He could not deny it. It awed, like the mystic ritual of all worship. There was the latest priest, who knew as usual of ciphers hidden from laymen, and he had the necessary dim religious light to make his ministration obscure. Seven candlesticks on an altar in a holy recess were not more subjecting than those vital half-hidden lustrous wheels railed off from sacrilege, and the gnomic switchboards with their glow-lamps.

The watching doubter at the window marvelled; but he was suspicious. How if Force be another of the jealous gods? As likely as not it is keeping its more important secrets. Man has exalted it. But does he know its unfulfilled endowment? He has made it the heart of his commune, the source of his light, and the reason for his labour and devotion. It is the Omnipotent on whom he calls to scatter his enemies; but perhaps like other inscrutable and ineffable gods it is mocking him with reservations it will disclose to no hierophant, no matter what the faith and fervour of worship, except in its own time. The fire stolen from Heaven was handy and docile in that original hollow tube of Prometheus, but it held chances beyond the guess of the first benefactor of man. The tube is blowing great guns and small arms now. Man contrived to steal power from the gods, but, the fool he is, he forgot to bring with it the clue to its right use, and here is Chaos come again.

Travers declined in instinctive revulsion the hypnotizing paraphernalia of Force. It was not so genial as Astarte and her occasions. Without a doubt, when we bow down to anything for what we hope to gain by it, then we must take whatever belongs to it; and the devil may be in it. He felt his way in the shadows beyond the window's lane of light, concerned only with abstractions, and stumbled over a limp bundle on the pavement.

He struck a match. A woman gaped up at it, an aged and vacant face. She stared, with no resentment, no expectation, no hope, made no sign that now she was surprised by a visitor who would have good tidings; and then, without a complaint, bent her tousled grey head on her rags again, to sleep, sitting with her back to the wall of the power-house.

Chapter Thirteen

HE WANDERED ON. THE TRUTH, HE BEGAN TO CONJEC-
ture, was that he was trying to walk away from himself, to step off his shadow. Presently weariness made
him halt. He sighed. Where was he?

The stars, he noticed, were becoming faint, and he
sympathized; he had been out all night himself, and
was not feeling too strong. They had changed position, too, and he could not at once name them, as
though he had walked far enough to get the constellations upside down. There was the east, the brightening
wall. He could not see what advantage he had gained,
except that he was outside the city. It was open land.
Another day was just about to enter the scene, but the
earth did not know it yet, and was still asleep, huddled
and indistinct. It had no settled form, except a gasometer and some factory shafts in the east. What looked
like a sleeping animal was near, but he found it was a
wheelbarrow. He made a seat of that.

Most of what was left of night in the sky was a

planet. The bands of Orion had been loosed, and the hunter had gone. Travers rested his head in his hands. Who was it said that we cannot loose the bands of Orion? Why, anybody might do it. He might have done it himself that night. You can't tell what stellar rift may be started by a simple dodge here below with the wrong bent. That's the trouble. You can't be sure the balance of the Galaxy is absolutely no concern of ours. A yaup of human infelicity to jar the song the morning stars sing together—to put them out of tune? Possibly. Nobody knows! The universal riddle, with unlucky Mr. Jones scratching his head over it in a suburban backyard, had best be considered as no empty joke of an idiot. It may have a gist. There may be a light beyond our telescopes whither all is destined, even if we don't like our particular path which leads we don't know where. And there may be no reason anywhere in it; but, if there is not, then let men, for the fun of it, show the vast lunacy of stars a point of genuine light.

He looked round again, and guessed he had been nodding. He shivered. The filmy shroud about him was beginning to fall into reasonable shapes, and the air was as clear and cold as glass, and as still. The earth must be on the point of rousing. He could smell its sweat. Well, it had a sound body, to smell as musky as that. But there was no stir yet. The very breathing of the place seemed to have stopped, just before it sat up and began anew.

Here it came. A party of little round-faced clouds had seen the sun, and were choristers. Anyhow, they seemed to be singing; a shower of shrill rays fell from them, flickering slivers of sound, a quavering of buoyant recitative. A skylark was up and about his business.

Travers did not move. He watched the dawn climb the tiers of the firmament, and looked for the singer in the glow. A dog barked far away, a minute voice, with all the empty land to itself. Then the sun peered over the rim of the world, and the shadows stretched out in a field of cabbages; there he was, sitting among a suitable congregation of cow-cabbages.

He was amused, but also greatly surprised. He had never suspected cabbages of easy competence in an accord with daybreak. Here superbly they were, and evidently it was all one to them whether their field was in Lancashire or the Hesperides. For a moment in the day even cabbages could rejoice, as though they were blithe skylarks. No doubt about it, the wings of Psyche had not a brighter tincture than the whorls and volutes of these vegetables, unless her wings were happier than translucent emerald, ruby and zircon. This fodder beat all the Ionic capitals. It had its own radiance, and at two a penny.

Now another bird was up, singing over this field. Had it a surer divination than most men? Its song did not falter in a melancholy minor because morning is soon over and music is mortal. It was without intellectual doubt. It was not brave. It only kept the tradition of its kind; that would last, he guessed, while the sun could rise, and skylarks were there to meet it.

It was the frailest of tokens. But who needs to be convinced by the Himalayas? When you have the sign, that is all. Now he knew that if the traditions of what men had found to be good were neglected till they were no more than a chance reminder through the incidence of morning in the leaves of a vegetable, that hint must be kept, though the practical measures of insanity and industry had then disciplined all the green earth under asphalt and had filled common opinion with soot and grease. There would be the more reason then for remembrance. Hold fast to the last token! Whoever knows the hint must keep it. It may have to be rendered up.

And that would be the real revolution! It might start some day, in such a dawn as this. Men perhaps would rise, as happy as birds wakening to the sun, and laugh at the deformities which darkness had hidden, and clear the way. Begin anew. It must be believed— one had to hold fast to that, if it were only a notion, or else own up that the best is only a consoling lie, comeliness an accident, and so surrender to the ubiquity of the invulnerable beast without a mind.

Chapter Fourteen

NOT FOR HIM. NO SURRENDER TO AN AMORPHOUS AND
instinctive hulk of a beast! If a man must be in error,
let it be to the unknown god. Better to die in that than
to sweat cheerfully in the multitude.

Out of a plain of allotment gardens a footpath
brought Travers to a wide junction of roads. Now
which way? Nothing was there to make one highway
more like the narrow gate, for a careful chooser, than
the others. They were public roads for general pur-
poses. They were raw on both sides through a headlong extension of a city upon the fields. A limy mire
surrounded rising brickwork. There was a grievance of
overturned hedges and shabby grass, and dumps of arid
building material. Near him some elms stood amid the
hurry of the improvements, and their boles were worn
and hamstrung and blotched with mortar. Resting
against the nearest tree in a drunken way was a crumpled sheet of corrugated iron. A wagon, laden with
steel girders, was drawn close to the kerb, near Trav-

ers. Coupled to the wagon was a traction engine, and its glowing belly was dropping fiery ordure on the road.

Its young driver, relaxed as an athlete after an effort, had a fist resting on the glossy green flank of his engine, and was idly considering a bearing. His reeking giant was stronger than a drove of horses, but its master eyed it in measuring indifference. Travers felt a desire to greet him, but the engine-driver's pose betrayed the aristocrat, aware of his caste. He moved about his monster with the unconcern of perfect trust, his faith assured of the explosion clamped in its sizzling inside. His good-humoured blue eyes were all that was bright and clear about him; his greasy fist was firm and brown as a coconut, his lank straw-coloured hair neatly trimmed round a moist neck as sleek and tough as a bull's. When he bent to peer under his engine, his loose shirt showed the curves of his shoulders and back, and they satisfied Travers that they could rise easily, if slowly, under the weight of any oppression. It was a figure to suggest that young life everywhere has the original virtue of trees and birds. It promised that it could begin on something new at any time. It whistled. The morning belonged to it, and it rested a careless hand on the steel ribs of power. Very likely it could reject steel girders, or anything else which displeased it, with the change of a thought and the flick of a muscle; strike a match on its pants, light a cigarette, look cheerfully another way, and forget it.

A succession of trams was filling rapidly with early workmen. Travers wondered whether the spirit of life stood near invisibly, perhaps by that cast-iron lamp standard in the centre of the junction of roads, like a policeman on traffic duty, and directed each soul in the confluent welter of humanity to its task. The streaming mobs were loose, they cluttered along without form, but every man in them as he arrived went straight to his place. Streams of people were flowing down ordained channels to turn the wheels of the mills.

The spirit of life on point-duty? No fear of that. What is done through duty is dead. This inevitability of movement is an illusion. This massed tractability is not man's morning substitute for light and colour and songs of joy. Only the general stream is amorphous and mindless. Nothing but the mob flows unconsciously by gravity down habitual ways. What about that young engine-driver, with his cheerful and dangerous blue eye? He was there, and more like him. Form was inherent in that host. The streams of men always carry unpredictable hazards. One of the cloth caps bobbing along on that tide of living power, now unrecognizable, might have that magic under it which, when evoked, could deflect the habitual flow of the days. The chance was always present, bobbing along, morning after morning, adding to the general movement its mite of energy, though there were so many years of it, docile and undistinguished, that all the pundits were sure at last the pour of humanity in one profitable direction was as fated as the path of the asteroids. But don't you believe it. The assembled traction engines of the kingdom, all fuming, are nothing to one cloth cap. On a fine morning, not specially noted in the calendar, an unknown cap-wearer, merged with his fellows, has a touch of sun. He goes fey. That one point in the stream no longer bobs along the current. It stops and interrupts the regular flow; presently deflects it, dams it up convincingly, gathers the oncoming caps into a deepening threat, swells them into an irresistible opinion fed by all the rills of the countryside, and away goes a flood to alter the landscape for ever, and spin every wheel to another purpose. If that were not possible, humanity would be as dumb as a bed of oysters.

The engine-driver was satisfied that all was well with his charge. He strolled away from it to a coffee-stall, which stood a little back on the road-waste. It was then Travers fancied he smelt pleasant things; he remembered suddenly he was mortal. He was uncertain whether he would be welcomed at so exclusive a hostel, but he approached it. An audience of workers, in hurried refreshment before a zinc platform projecting breast-high from a movable shop, very like a Punch and Judy box, within which a man in shirt-sleeves presided at an urn, made way for him. They did not look at him, but acknowledged he was there by giving him space enough.

He hesitated with his order too long. A difficulty appeared at the table. Several seamen briskly arrived, and their frivolous remarks were in a kind of English, but their money was not understood at all; it was foreign.

The man in shirt-sleeves held their coins delicately in the palm of his hand, but in doubt and at arm's length, eyeing them over the top of his spectacles, as though he feared they would infect him. He then glanced at the new group.

"Whad yer call all this?"

One of the men leaned his arms genially on the counter, to show he had time to answer every question. "Well, mate, what do you call it?"

The stall-keeper arranged the coins carefully on the table before the seaman's weathered paws. "There you are," he said, "if you've lost any buttons."

The sailor picked them up slowly, and sighed. Travers had expected a noise, for that affronted man had the definition of one who would act abruptly, if hindered; but he only sighed. He turned candidly to his friends. "We've bumped again," he explained to them. "Have to go astern off this patch. No grub till we come to a shop where silver is silver. Shove off, boys."

Travers touched the man, and was met by a strictly enquiring stare which had not been given to the stall-keeper. "Don't go," said Travers. "It's a bit of a pull into town. Have it with me, won't you?"

"You'll pay?"

"That's it."

"What for?"

"I know it's a fair jaunt into town, if you must walk."

The seaman showed his surprise. It was hard to believe this. "Is that the tally?" he asked doubtfully. "Mister, if you've got no other reason, that's a good un. You can pay." He stood vigilant for a moment as though a deeper reason for this bounty might become apparent, then he signed his friends up to the counter.

"These fellers," he advised Travers apologetically, "are a bit weak in the head, if you know what I mean. They'd eat out of anybody's hand. I've known them trust a gang-plank that wasn't there. If you don't watch it they'd never see their wives, if they've got any."

"Are you in charge of them?"

"What, me? Bert Byles in charge of firemen and deckhands? No, mister. I don't know how to carry beer loose in my pocket. I'm only a bo'sun. If these chaps want a bit of gumption, I pass it on, same as you."

Mr. Byles stood with a mug of coffee in his hand, innocently leery, while he spoke, of this unusual visitor to an early-morning stall, as though conning the run of a new and interesting craft. He appeared to be satisfied. He raised his mug and respectfully clinked it against Travers'.

Chapter Fifteen

THOUGH BABEL—AND FANNY TRAVERS RECALLED THE
fact in surprise—had but one tower, it was cast down.
So a wrong sort of tower was noticeable from on high?
Perhaps Babel's tower was an especially awful confluent rising of sin. What about those peaks and turrets
before her now? But they were triumphant, though
appalling.

She was standing at a mid-air eyrie of New York,
swimming her sight, for the first time, over the immense uprising of Manhattan's towers in an exultant
morning light, a legion of towers, astonishing and
splendid, as though mustered for the assault of heaven's
escarpments. Her sight swam over that bright array in
conscious temerity. When it swooped earthward she
felt a little dizzy, like a bird whose wings are new to
it. A chasm dropped from her feet. How far it dropped
she did not dare to peep. Her hotel might lose its balance if she leaned forward.

This host of aspiring towers was audacious enough

to draw the jealous attention of the sentries of the sky. So bold a flaunting of the human will might catch the stern curiosity of Gabriel at any moment. While she was watching? To gaze, and have that suspicion at the same time, made her feel she was swooning outward. Her own standing was on the seventeenth story—or was it the seventieth?—much too high, anyhow, for a toppling through celestial wrath. The radiant presumption of the city was scarey. When she arrived last night she made the steep ascent to heaven from the ground floor for a full minute—was floating up swiftly all the way to the stars without a pause. Then the elevator decisively stopped. Perhaps it knew the exact place for her virtue. It would have been dangerous to let her rise any higher—that might have given away the whole show, revealed New York's daring invasion of the abode of the saints. When citizens live dangerously there is a greater need for exactitude. So she had to get out of the lift, and two scarlet fire-axes were crossed on the wall right before her, a nasty reminder that she had to do better yet before she was allowed to go higher; or were they only the city's scarlet symbol of a common fear? Watch and pray in this city; we are all asking for it!

Here she was in New York. She wished she knew

precisely what to do there. She pondered that, her sight wandering amid the buoyant confusion of luminous spires and bastions that had filaments of cirrus, pennants of vapour drifting across them, down to the bottom of a narrow gorge in the mid-distance, which diminished to a line in perspective, with insects of various shapes crawling along the floor of it. Her sight hovered hopelessly before an infinitude of dots, which were windows perforating geometrically vistas of pale precipices. Threescore and ten years were not long enough for her to fly along every parapet of this city, and down and across every vast parallelogram of windows, till at last she peered into one pane of glass and saw John within; if he were there, that is.

What made Mantell think he was? She could hear frequent rumblings at the foot of her own cliff, as if an earthquake were trying to begin, but found the city very heavy; and hysterical whistles, and an occasional grating screech. If she continued to stare into that upper tumultuous brightness any longer she'd let out a screech herself. Though that would not help her; it would not grate on anybody. The world was magnificently and riotously mad, so it was no use trying to put right one little thing in it, though that were only a lost husband. First of all John very surprisingly appeared in a ship out of the blue, when she doubted that the blue knew anything of him; there he was, at the appointed hour, standing in an alphabetical shed under the letter T. She learned that he was carefully indexed in the book of life. But now where was he? For she had picked up a newspaper, and when she had put it down he was dissolved into the blue again. . . .

The telephone! Telephones in Babel? Who knew she was here?

"Yes"—"Yes, I am"—"Who? I didn't catch your name"—"Mr. Kirk?"—"Oh, Mr. Quirke! So sorry"—"What?"—"Of course"—"Did you know him? Do you know where he is?"—"No, I don't"—"What is it you want?"—"All right, I must see you then"—"Say it slowly, while I write down your address."

She thrust down the instrument with such careless promptitude that it fell over. Its plaintive protest steadied her. Scandalous to be rude with it, after what it had done! She picked it up and made it comfortable with care, her hand shaking. The delicate thing had to be set in friendly adjustment to chaos, as it could pick up voices that would answer your thoughts.

Quirke; who was he? She had never heard of him before. She frowned over his name, at the balcony, with the upper confusion of New York before her, but now unseen. A queer name! It did not sound suitable, but it would not have come out of the air without reason. Even our telephones are all numbered.

She trusted the name was altogether reasonable. Reason, she hoped, might be getting the best of it everywhere now and had begun to put her own house in order again. Time it did, too. If reason could only arrest John, and hold him tight till she got there! After all, the alphabetical shed had properly indexed him, and she found him in the right place at once, so it was but fair to the world to suppose that it was John who was wrong; he had lost his tag. Now there was a chance she could tie it on him again. But could he be back in New York, after the way he had abused it? Such an idea was like a prompt total eclipse. She shrank from it. If he were really in that city again, then something might be worse than even the fact that she had lost him briefly. Mantell may have been right, after all. Poor John possibly had worked loose a screw, through running his brain too hard on empty air. That he had shipped back to a place he didn't like, as though he had just left his pipe there, was enough to prove it.

No. It was better not to dwell on that. There was

enough work cut out, to find him, and here a door was opening. The sudden release of hope made her feel buoyant. The notion seized her that she could even float out of the hotel by that window—blow over the balcony—descend to the street obliquely and spirally like thistledown. But perhaps it would be unwise to trust oneself too freely to words of gossamer; the usual elevator was more advisable.

Her taxicab made swift intermittent spurts along Fifth Avenue. She got from it freakish upward glimpses of a strange panorama when the wheels of the cab were not screaming in hysterical recoils from imminent collisions, for which she braced herself, shutting her eyes. It would be unimportant if she were killed. She accepted that. This place was too remarkable to pay attention to little things. Quite right. Let little people enjoy themselves in their own way, if they are ready to pay the price.

For she felt the usual elation and capriciousness of a newcomer to Manhattan. She had become younger in a night. Grudging old Europe couldn't stop her now. It was all true, then—happily you could begin again in America. (Surely John hadn't come here to do that, and without her?) She observed the people

on the sidewalks intently, especially the women. They
were not meek. They were perfectly assured top-dogs.
She doubted whether they so much as knew of under-
dogs. She relished the challenge of their cool and slow
arrogance. Breathing the air of a new earth had that
extraordinary effect on people. She felt herself as if
she had been drinking wine; but in New York you
didn't need it. This place gave the impression of a tre-
mendous spree. It was a wonder the pavements kept
still, that they did not respond to the banners above,
and float about. Sober notions went wild in New
York, as though they'd had a drop too much. Even
the buildings were out for a lark.

The brakes of her cab screamed again as it missed
death, and looking out of the window as she composed
herself—the cab was resting for a minute, after its
fright—she saw a Georgian house. It was finished yesterday, by the newness of it, in Quaker bricks tem-
perately red, and window-frames of a dark green; a
chaste old idea out of Hampstead gone frivolously
drunk to the very clouds, waving a flag aloft and daring the sky to come down.

And there was a church, the first she had seen! It
surprised her, for somehow she was not expecting to

see a church. Well, they'd put the old English God in his inferior place here, without a touch of tender remorse. He didn't count. They couldn't sack him, for family reasons, but they weren't going to give him much room. She felt homesick and sorry because of that church, though it was only dingy Gothic of the late Baptist period. But it stood so meekly between two great free-and-easy banks, its tiny spire raised no higher than their lower windows, as if pleading to them, like an orphan lifting its hands to the waistcoat buttons of big rich uncles, who wouldn't look down; they had no time for orphans. Poor little church! Now, she hoped, she'd see a church to the American God. That would be cyclopean, terrific, with awful storms bulging across its middle, as on Everest. That church would have to top even the roof of the world, for it would be raised to a very, very large God, the biggest of all.

If John showed any desire to remain in New York she had a reckless idea that she would encourage him. As an architect, he could break loose from the tuppenny standards and prohibitions of Europe. He could let himself go. He could be born again, and build for people who wouldn't look more than twice if you went beyond the snow line.

Lord, here was such a building! The cab had stopped. Surely this was not the address Mr. Quirke had given? She questioned the taxi-man anxiously.

He was indifferent; he did not look round at her. He was chewing. "Yeah!" he said.

Chapter Sixteen

SHE FALTERED IN DOUBT BEFORE THE AUSTERE PORTAL
of that structure. If it was the right size for the right
people she feared she would be lost in it. Its summit
was out of sight. What was behind those doors of
bronze and crystal did not know her life. They chal-
lenged her humble errand. The men of that tower
would bend to her whispering as though she had come
to a cathedral about a lost umbrella. She could not believe anybody was there named Quirke. What sort of
inhabitants would they be? Would they speak her
language?

Once within the doors she did not dare to use English. It would not be encouraged. Nobody there was
speaking. They were not giving anything away. She
was expected to find out. It was a great hall with a
surround of noiseless spider-web doors incessantly
opening and folding, enclosing men in cages which
vanished instantly aloft; or releasing them from cages
in bunched and precipitous departures, men whose

common expression of severity and repentance left no doubt that they had learned on a floor near the sky all there was to know about themselves, and with bowed heads were now hurrying to inform dear friends they were done for. She watched them in awe. These were the world-famous American men of business. Even John had heard of them. And what strange men they were! They were all alike. They must all eat the same food in unison, without seeing it, and it disagreed with them. With their timid eyes, prim lips, and drained and translucent cheeks, they might have been elderly and finical spinsters in trousers. They did not see her there. They had enough to worry them.

This bare hall she was in was of black marble and white metal so highly polished and sanitary that not a miserable fly could hide anywhere in it. She guessed it was taken from a book by H. G. Wells. She didn't know in which of the metallic spider-webs she would be caught, if she asked for it, and shrank from asking. She sought a stairway. There wasn't one. There was no chance of a personal and ignorant escape out of it. She had to speak at last to a uniformed half-negro, who was on the point of ascension. He motioned her into his lift with a casual backward movement of his head. That cage was nearly full of sad and silent men, who

reverently and together took off their hats as she joined
them. They knew. She was going to be a helpless suf-
ferer like themselves, and they knew it, without being
told.

After a swift flight the lift paused. She waited. Nobody moved in the cage. The men observed her slyly.
She was embarrassed, but enduring. Then the half-
negro turned reproachful eyes to her and motioned her
out of it. So here was destiny for her. She was abandoned in a long and luminous corridor, and was alone
in it except for distant figures which erupted from
hidden openings and disappeared straight in others.
Their swift transits were certainly on business, and of
life or death. She began an aimless walk, for luck.
Where the chances were so many it was startling to
come upon the door in which she had barely believed,
International Concessions, Incorporated.

Her appearance within the office was met instantly
by a loud fusillade from a regiment of elegant stenogra-
phers, all haughty and quick at their machines. The
concessions, she thought, must be many and rich,
which those typewriters were trying at continuously
high speed to overtake. She stood patiently at a low
mahogany barrier. She hoped one of the girls would
catch a concession quickly, and then come to her. No-

body noticed her, though she knew she must be dreadfully conspicuous. She knew she was of less consequence than concessions, whatever they might be. Now she humbly realized also that she resembled less a mythical Parisienne than any one of these young women; naturally they must give her plenty of time to understand that. When this period had thoroughly elapsed one of them approached her in nonchalance.

Next she was in a waiting-room, where worrying thoughts were the only noises not absorbed by the dense pile of a Chinese carpet, and the dusky oak panelling, which was not antique, but might have been. Presently another door opened, and somebody said he was Mr. Quirke. "Come in, Mrs. Travers." He noticed her astonishment as she entered the apartment beyond. It was baronial. "This," Mr. Quirke explained to her, "is the board room."

No board was there. What a board it must be when it was present, and how vitally necessary that it should never forget that its discussions were of grave and ponderous matters! The board could never forget that. The masonry of a new capacious Elizabethan recess for a fire enclosed the latest shining novelty in electric heaters. A brass candelabrum, which was not antique but might have been, carrying a constellation of electric bulbs, like an inverted and symmetrical tree full of fruit, was doubled in the lustre of a massive mahogany table so prolonged that a man, who was sitting at the far end of it, was small and lonely. There was a double array of solemn chairs beside the table, as consequential as thrones, and all empty but one. It was quite a walk to the other end of the mahogany, to where the little man was lonely.

She hardly believed the room; she did not believe the name of the little man. It was Snarge. True, lords often have funny names. And on the instant she fell melancholy, because she understood that such a room, and two such men, could know nothing whatever of John. It wasn't natural. All this was forlornly alien. You could have seen the least speck of hope on the polish of that table, had it been there.

Then they were talking to her. Her fluttered attention soon became still, and settled upon the pair of them. What on earth were they talking about so politely!

Did she know New York! And how did she like it, as far as she had got! And was it better than London . . . Paris. Perhaps she preferred Italy . . . Rapallo . . . Rome!

No? Of course, people went even to Moscow now,

for pleasure. They were watching her, too, as if they scarcely believed her. She told them she had not come to America to compare her travel experiences.

They assured her they knew she had not. At every answer she made in cool and puzzled indifference they watched her as though her words were artful mice peeping out of a dim corner, and they were afraid they'd see no more than quivering whiskers. That fellow Snarge had a smile which loitered on his face while you spoke, as if to let you see that though he was tired he was not displeased to meet you, but that he knew most people's words were spurious. He hardly spoke, though. He was the listener. But Mr. Quirke was full of oblique curiosity.

She became impatient. "Why did you telephone to me, Mr. Quirke?"

He recovered quickly from that, and was candid. "I wanted you to tell us where your husband is. I thought you would, when you knew that it would be better for him if we heard." He was even playful. His nervously twitching eye and wry mouth suggested, preposterously, that he was both artful and friendly. "If you're in town, I'm quite sure he can't be far off."

Mrs. Travers leaned forward, as if to see him closer,

and then slowly rose. The two men were unaware that they, too, must rise, but surprise, as they noted the frowning astonishment of their visitor, brought even his lordship to his feet.

"You are sure he isn't far off? Your interest is very kind. Why do you want to know where he is?"

"Now, now, now," said Mr. Quirke. "You surely know that. You know why we ask that."

She turned to his lordship. "What has my husband to do with you?"

His lordship was deprecatory. His kind smile lingered, and he indicated Quirke as one who could explain.

"It's all right, Mrs. Travers," said Quirke, in mocking resignation to her pride. "I met your husband in Liverpool, the day he got back from America. You've heard of that. You can't expect me to believe you know nothing about that. Lord Snarge hasn't seen him—not yet—but let me tell you that they'd better not meet. Your husband's interest in his lordship's business is too close, and it isn't wanted. Where is he now?" Mr. Quirke's mouth took an ironic twist. "Anyhow, tell him from me to keep out, wherever he is."

"What is his lordship's business?"

"Mrs. Travers, that's all we've got to say to you. He'd better keep out. Men in business don't like having their interests meddled with. It makes trouble. You understand what I mean?"

"Not a bit. I don't believe you know my husband. May I ask why he saw you in Liverpool, and what happened?"

Mr. Quirke smiled, and glanced at his lordship, as if to indicate that there was the sort of wife to have.

"I want to know—I must know. What had he to do with you in Liverpool? I haven't seen him since."

Mr. Quirke inclined his head in respectful acquiescence. "I didn't say you had. It wouldn't surprise me if you hadn't. It isn't so long ago."

Quirke, as he watched for the effect of this, became uneasy. Her slight figure was pressed back against the table, her hands behind it for support. Her poise suggested tension; that and her silence made him wonder what would happen next. She was doing this very well. Too well? Was he mistaken? She might have been in a trance, staring at him that way. Anyone would think he was horrible. Quirke moved under her still inspection, and broke the spell. There might be something in this, he was thinking. After all, she was only a girl.

"Mrs. Travers . . ." he began, quietly; but a lifetime of astuteness put the note of guile in his voice, even when doubt now made it hesitant. She swept them off with a gesture, and went from that room as though in fear of what was there.

Chapter Seventeen

IT WAS IN THAT YEAR, NOT SO FELICITOUS AS THIS, when men in all lands, if we except the northern extremity of Greenland and Penguinia of the Antarctic, had ceased to believe at last the genius of their rulers was doing them much good.

Perhaps the country of Paranagua might be another exception. There it is too hot, and malaria too potent, for a man to remain an ardent rebel longer than a morning argument with the aperitif. A politician unjustly excluded from the administration of Paranagua soon loses his patriotic indignation in the humid heat, for the equatorial forest and the Indians are at the end of a tram ride through its only city, and so he becomes exhausted before his bribe. It was in that year, now forgotten by a younger generation whose happy world is ruled in wisdom, when not a statesman anywhere, from Japan to Washington, and so across to Geneva through London and Paris, though he did no more than allow an interview to a journalist, but increased the anxiety of his helpless people, in an effort to soothe it; because in those days it had been learned that when a statesman spoke with kindly assurance of good it was a token that the worst was still to come.

In such a year a steamer rounded Salado Point into the Rio Javari, and anchored off Santa Maria, which is the capital of Paranagua. She was no more than something to watch. Steamers are not unusual at Santa Maria, where they call perhaps once a week, when collecting bananas, timber, and coffee, about the neighbouring coasts and islands. She approached slowly, for the volume of the Javari, bringing to the sea the melted snows of ranges that from Santa Maria are but an infrequent surmise in the heavens, is broad and powerful, the burden of a continental drainage.

The steamer was watched from the shore with close but indolent interest, except by Mr. Glenthorpe, the British Minister, who heard her syren, looked up from his desk, failed to recognize her, and wondered. Nobody else who saw her was at work when she rounded the Point; and besides, whatever one was doing could wait, when a steamer was entering the Javari. An incoming ship, to the people of Santa Maria, was a communication from a lively and a daylight world. She was the occasion of most of the authentic news. That other world, behind them, faded quickly into conjecture. Sounds came from it, and rumours, and occasionally a traveller, but not much that was tangible except the bi-weekly train from the mining region of Zaraza. The magnitude of it, and an insufficiency of particulars, inspired lofty thoughts in full and momentous periods whenever Paranaguans were orating in public assembly. For Paranagua beyond Santa Maria had the attraction of a mystery, about which almost anything may be said. Nobody who desired to publish his knowledge of it knew much about it, and that accounted for the occasional sensational stories, some of which were good enough to be cabled to America and Europe. There were even books about Paranagua, eloquent of rich but undeveloped chances, hinting broadly at marvels of lost cities that to archæologists were more than curious, and at sinister political intrigues too bad even for secrets of diplomacy.

The mystery was notable. It was especially attractive to a newcomer when, beyond the somnolence of Santa Maria's brief wharves, and the palisades about it of the forest, which appeared to confine it to the river under an overhanging weight of foliage, he was surprised by a far apparition in the sky. He saw the lower reach of the Javari contract in perspective into the

south-west, a long resplendent mirror framed by the
sombre wilderness, and above and beyond where it
dwindled into the interior was a vision, which he knew
could not be of tinctured cloud, yet ought not to be
land at that altitude, and of those colours, and with
nothing beneath it. The Sierras! But by the time he had
turned in astonishment to point the appearance to his
neighbour it had dissolved into the vague and general
legend.

It was then that he began to suspect that more might
come from that direction than could arrive from seaward. The land expanded. Imagination began to enrich
it. That was the fascination of Paranagua, especially
to those watchful interests in Wall and Threadneedle
Streets, which are very sensitive, and always regret any
waste of the natural beauties of the earth; and it is
true that the forests, savannahs, and mountains of Paranagua, with their oil and ore, are squandered on sun-
sets and sunrises, and on a people whose Latin pride,
though freely adulterated with the stoic indifference of
the Indian and the unwitting indolence of the negro,
is content with Paranagua as it is, if to alter it would
exact labour and the beginnings of worry; and a pride,
too, which respects nothing in the energetic Anglo-
Saxon but his money.

The steamer anchored. A man descended from her bridge and entered a cabin beneath it. The white launch of the Customs was already skimming round her as a swift and glossy water-beetle does about a log. John Travers and Bert Byles, amongst others, were watching the newcomer in the stream, but without comment. They were observing the ship out there, and the bo'sun recognized a familiar shape, and noted the salt which was crusted on her smokestack, and the rust streaked from her bows; she had had a dusting, he thought, but he said nothing. They were looking at her because the rumble of her descending cable had interrupted their amiable difference over another matter.

The bo'sun was advising Travers. He cocked his thumb over his shoulder at all Paranagua. "Leave that alone. Don't do it. I feel weak, mister, when I lose sight of water. That's how it is. I'm going to be lost when I turn my back on this wharf. It's like this. If you go up there, I got to. But I ask you. Take another look at this country—if it is a country. What's in it? Thieves and stinks, as near as I can make it. I know what to do with thieves, when I'm paying attention, but these local flavours ain't natural, not like bilge. They'd take the enamel off a mess-tin, and they follow me about. What about my inside?" The bo'sun's face was studiously dolorous, and Travers enjoyed it.

"There's my inside, too."

"Is there? Well, it's yours, if you've got one." Bert Byles was doubting that his wardenship of his companion would avail, if he got out of his reckoning, and that made him diplomatic. "I hear they got yellow fever here, too." He had a Cockney's contemptuous dubiety of the unusual in Latin countries.

Travers was watching the port officials climbing the ladder on the ship's side. He nodded to that scene. "There's a chance, bo'sun, out there. Why not take it?"

"Now then, Mr. Travers, that won't do. Desert, you say. Nice idea for a gentleman, that is. Chuck it when you're sorry for yourself. Do I look like a sailor with a hard-luck story for the night porter of a sailor's home?"

"From what I know of you, if you had such a story he'd take it. But you'll die at sea."

"Glad to hear you say it. That's what bothers me. I can't see it, the way you're going."

"Well, that's the way it goes just now. I'm glad you're here, but I didn't ask you to come. I knew what it would be like."

"You did? Not you. You never thought twice about it. What's more, you'd be wrong if you had. Facts don't matter to you." The sailor began to mumble. He had something else to say, but it was really serious, and so he was shy. "Some things you know all right, but I don't. They're different. You can find bearings where I can't see a mark, and I'll steer any course you set. I suppose you're right, somehow." The bo'sun thrust out his lower lip plaintively with that regrettable admission. Then he brightened. "I won't say I'm not a fool, mister, off and on, if you know what I mean. Didn't I sign on for a trip like this? I did, just to see where it came out. But it's asking for trouble. I know that damwell, and you don't."

"There's trouble on any course."

"My grandmother told me that, when I first went to sea. It made her cry. That's why I went. Trouble goes down in the articles. We're paid to get round it. But what are you doing? Here you are, laying a course that'll fetch hell."

"That's nothing to do with us."

"What? Nothing? My oath it ain't. But won't we be there? When it comes down to it, you gentle Jesus fellers are worse than any Welsh shipowner. He can be scared stiff, if he knows somebody's got a picture

131

postcard to send to the underwriters. But once you get an idea in your head you keep on and on, and you'd make a blackmailer seem like a nice, kind mission lady. How was I to know what you were talking about, those first days in Liverpool? I could only see there was no money in it. Fact is, I'd never met a man before all lit up over a job of work that wouldn't pay. I wondered what was in the charter, as you could see it all, as plain as a masthead light I couldn't pick up. What was it? Dunno. Here we are."

"Not for long."

"Mr. Travers, there was only one thing in your talk I could see easy enough to hold on to. What did you know of men and women? Nothing. Not enough to count your change at a coffee stall."

"And that is why you came along?"

"Did you hear me say it?"

"Not a word like it. But I have noticed your respect for them isn't like mine."

"You haven't been a bo'sun."

"Well, it has held them off, when I've worried because they were coming too close."

The steamer's syren blared, and the surprise of it burst a flock of parrots from the tree-tops of the opposite shore like the stars of a rocket. Travers idly watched the stars descend. The bo'sun watched the steamer. He grumbled.

"What's she want."

"Do you know her?"

"Know her? That's the old *Cairngorm*. Do I know her! You told me she was my chance. She's not a chance, she's a mistake. I wonder what she's doing here. You're going to see the British consul or somebody, didn't you say? Ask him, for me. It'll be a bit of news I can understand, all this way from home. She's off her usual run here. She's been a long time coming, too, by the look of her."

Chapter Eighteen

ANOTHER MAN WAS CONSIDERING THE *Cairngorm* IN the distance. Mr. Glenthorpe, the British Minister, could see her from his desk, without rising.

In Santa Maria he rarely knew what next to expect, but the vagaries of men attracted him, though they never disturbed him; he accepted the wet with the fine days, and neither praised nor blamed. Nor would he ever rise, unless that effort were imperative. It was easy to infer, from his restful pose, that he was absent-minded, and the ship newly arrived had happened to come before his eyes, or that the still heat was weari-some, and he was not inclined to work, and so had taken an indifferent excuse to drop it.

Strangers could easily make that mistake when they met Mr. Glenthorpe, and perhaps he encouraged them to it. It helped the work of his mission. His post was not endangered by cunning and tact. Yet visitors ad-mired him, too, though most of them suspected that he was somewhat too elegant and personable, and that his leisured manner was an added affectation. It restored self-esteem to reflect that his patrician mask was as if carved in wood. His intelligence would be slow. After their first surprise, as Mr. Glenthorpe welcomed them, because his presence made them acutely conscious of their inferior height, they were amused and assuaged to note, as they looked up to him, that he was just the pretty picture of what a British Minister should be but rarely is. It was for that reason foreigners felt more at ease with him than his own countrymen; they at once decided they could trust him. But a traveller from London, arriving in importance expanded by a familiarity with Whitehall, might feel a little flat and diminished in a brief interview with his nation's representative at Santa Maria, and hardly know why. Occasionally such a traveller was resentful, though there was nothing for him to complain about, even when he did complain in London, dropping a word in the place from which it might go on to take a little of the conceit out of that chap at Santa Maria.

Mr. Glenthorpe was wondering exactly where the steamer below fitted into life's local and attractive bewilderment. She was not the usual fruit ship. He had never seen her before. Had she a part in that game in the background designed to upset the dear old President and his circle, and bring in a new mob more amenable to the desires of the important alliances of a busier world outside? He hoped not, but he was afraid it was so. However, he wasn't supposed to have heard of that. He knew, of course, a great deal about several subjects, though a chance visitor would never guess so much information was in the room; the well-sustained fatigue in Mr. Glenthorpe's glance and voice were misleading, and thus a careless observer easily forgot that a man with such a nose is never tired, and that he must have followed it in bland inquiry into many unsuspected places during a fairly long life. His interests were unusual and diverse, and a guest was not likely to become aware of more than one of them. There was recently the brilliant and entertaining young zoologist from Oxford, Mr. Overall, who proposed to study the birds of Paranagua. Glenthorpe delighted him. The Minister's inconsequential asides on the popular literary and political figures at home were so near the hidden mark, though evidently innocent and at random; and not publishable, unluckily, for Mr. Overall proposed to write a witty and provocative book about his tropical experiences.

And another thing—though the peculiarity of it did

not occur to the young naturalist till he was back at the Hotel La Paz changing his clothes—where did Glenthorpe get all that original stuff about so remote and strange a fowl as the hoatzin; and how had he picked up that fund of native lore about the royal bird, the quezal? Very curious. There was, the same week, Mr. Van den Berg, of New York, who had supposed, before his visit, that he had nothing more to learn of guns and big game. He desired to bag a black jaguar, and thereupon was told where one was likely to be found, and the right way to get him; Mr. Glenthorpe showed himself to be not uninterested. The Britisher, so it seemed, had been far afield, and now the last big ibex in the Tien Shan would not draw him there again, nor the last rhinoceros to India. Mr. Van den Berg was sure that he had never met a better man. What about coming with him after this black tiger?

The Minister's wish to know more of the *Cairngorm* overcame his lassitude. He fancied he knew why she was there, and it was desirable that he should get as near the truth as he could. Who were the people about her deck? Santa Maria would suit him for a little while longer; the prospect of English winters, bridge parties, and golf, was depressing; and if this revolution began to move before he could guess the way it would go he might have to leave a country which was far enough away from the dear homeland to be acceptable.

Mr. Glenthorpe went to a telescope, which stood on a tripod by the veranda. From there he looked down over a descending shrubbery to where the roofs of the town were only small red rafts in a lower surf of foliage. The roofs were scattered about the cathedral, as though moored near an upstanding limestone rock. From that ledge on the hillside the river was a broad and resplendent lower road of quicksilver, and the shore opposite, the island of Guajara, uninhabited except by jaguars, peccaries, and fugitives from Santa Maria's substitute for justice, was a green cliff of uniform height in which pale isolated tree boles were pilasters and buttresses of silver. The distinction of those individual columns, and the splendour of the river, were ominously explicit then, for the afternoon storm was gathering; the background to Guajara was a sky like doom almost to the zenith, though the sun was displaying the still forest, pronouncing it inauspicious, ghastly and enchanted. Set centrally in the reflecting mirror of the river was the steamer. He slewed the telescope, and was patiently inspecting her, when

Mr. Travers was announced. He did not move. "Bring him in," he said to the telescope.

He knew that a queer Englishman named John Travers was in the town, with an attendant. The attendant had attracted too much unpleasant notice. He had broken a marble table in a saloon, one night, by banging it with a bull-fighter, locally much admired, who had ventured to puff a mouthful of cigarette smoke into a British face which met with his disapproval. Mr. Glenthorpe, when he heard of it, was charmed; it was not the thing for a Minister to do, but he was inclined to send for the indiscreet man, to warn him of danger, and also in curiosity about his arms and chest, because that bull-fighter was not a fellow to be tackled frivolously in his favourite saloon, with his adoring girls about him. As to Travers himself, Glenthorpe supposed that newcomer to be one of the cranks. Paranagua, with its uncertainties, had the usual fascination for cranks. They never failed to visit him, in their quest of rare sympathy, and he enjoyed them, as a rule, much more than the less frequent interviewers from home whose only aberration was their estimate of their consequence. He had an idea that Travers might be actually gaga. So much the better, unless he was of the simple variety which

owned the only diagram that showed precisely where
to plunge a spade into the secret treasure of Manoa.
The dotty treasure-hunters were more terrible bores
than the new industrial barons.

A monocle, at the end of a ribbon of black silk,
could be delicately rhetorical between Mr. Glenthorpe's finger and thumb when a visitor was greeted
in that room; occasionally the glass itself was used, for
it could promptly alleviate symptoms that betokened
a tendency to fellowship too eager and intimate.
When he turned and saw Travers, however, he did
not use it, even rhetorically. The two men, in a brief
strict appraisal across the room, disarmed their minds.
"Sorry if I'm troubling you. I've no concern with
secrets of state."

"None here worth mentioning, Mr. Travers. Er
. . . it only this moment occurs to me . . . your
name . . . I remember a war-memorial at home. Old-
castle's. I was looking at it a month or two ago. Tell
me, do you know the artist?"

"I do." Travers was gratified. That memorial had
been a gift, and he had given all he knew. "Perhaps,"
said Travers, "you noticed the Alcazar Hotel, while
you were home. There was a deal of stuff about it in

the press, at the same time. Do you prefer the memorial?"

"Much more." (Nothing gaga about this man, so far.)

"That's worth hearing. Nobody else does. Let it be a secret between us."

"What are you doing here?"

"You are direct to the mark."

"Sometimes it's better. . . . By the way, I ought to tell you that man of yours is sure to get into a mess, if he is so impulsive, and stays long."

"Byles? He can take care of himself, while taking care of me. We shall not stay long. You'd like him."

"I fancy I should. But advise him, for your sake, as he doesn't seem to care about his own carcass, not to be freely visible. I want to hear, too, whether that ship just in interests you, because of anything you've heard about her?"

Travers glanced carelessly at her. "No. I've heard nothing. Byles says he knows her. He's a sailor. He wondered why she was here, and asked me to find out."

"I've been wondering. It's as well to know. I'm afraid she means a rumpus. Some people here are expecting the fireworks to start the jollification, and it wouldn't surprise me if she has the consignment they want. This town may become noisy. What attracted you to Santa Maria?"

Travers smiled. "I've no part in it. I don't think I'd take a gun to shoot the devil."

"No. You'd only ginger him up if you did. Always leave that gentleman alone."

"Yes? You think we should let the devil have his way? I'm looking for Lord Snarge, if you want to know."

Mr. Glenthorpe glanced sideways at his visitor, and then his body moved with some mirth which made no other sign. "He was here not long ago."

"So I heard. I hoped he was here still. I've been following him about, but I don't seem able to catch him. Hasn't he gone up country?"

"It wouldn't do for me, officially, to help you to shoot him, but he did go inland."

"Then I'm after him. I promise you not to hurt him. All I want is a word with him. I'm trying to put a spoke in one of his wheels. I'll stop that part of his machinery, if I can. How did he strike you? Do you think anything can be done with him?"

"Done with him? I don't know what you want to do with him. You've only ruled out shooting. He's not easy to get at. He is not really a person. It struck me he was more the moving spirit of the age than a person. I wouldn't like to swear he is unconcerned with the doings which make this land a problem for me, and full of hope for important outsiders. At the same time, I can't swear that he is. Caution won't hurt you, if you want to stop a transaction of his which he intends to succeed. He has interests here, as well as elsewhere. And power. Lots of it." Mr. Glenthorpe lit a cigarette. "Lots of power. Look out! He doesn't need faith to shift mountains. He has wires. He can get them pulled to shift a row of mountains. The farther ends of his wires are in places where you'd be surprised to find them."

"I've been slowly learning that."

"Yes, it takes time, and you never know all. The captains and the kings have departed—or most of them, and I suppose the others are getting ready to back up—and now we must bow to gentlemen like his lordship. They rule, but have no thrones, so it isn't easy to upset them. You never know where to find them, yet wherever you turn you run into the holy privilege of usury, with its contracts and bonds more sacred today, as far as I know, than the word of God ever was. To interfere with them rouses what used to be called righteous wrath."

Travers, surprised by so much from so still a figure, lifted his head to read his host's face. It might have been that of Pharaoh, who had nothing to learn of rule. "Are you speaking of the devil, whose name is Legion? I've been moved by the hope that his lordship is vulnerable and mortal—even open to persuasion."

"Mortal? I don't know. I'm not sure about it. Very likely his name is Legion, too. What is mortality? I think we'd better see him as the origin of movements of life with which you and I must go, then we'll be nearer the mark." Glenthorpe lifted his hand and turned it about as though idly examining it as a suitable holder of his cigarette. "Is he mortal? Tell me, where's the end of those movements he starts? And you think he is open to persuasion! What of it? Once he has given the right assortment of things the proper touch, off they go, and he himself can't stop them. There he is, one of those men of action our schoolmasters told us to admire. You may now admire him! After all, what's wrong with him? He's as right as wireless telegraphy and high finance; as right as all the fine modern things. You've heard of something called the organization of our resources? That's old Snarge. If you think it is open to persuasion, try it!"

The shadow of the coming storm was deepening in the room. Travers could scarcely discern the forest across the river, until a pulsing of bluish light brought to view uncertainly, as though a theatrical backcloth were shaking, a line of chimerical trees.

Phantoms! As phantom as his lordship, and all his works. He, and they, too, wavered on the verge, between reality and nothing. They depend on what light there is. Patience possessed Travers, like the assurance of a power that was timeless.

Glenthorpe, too, was watching those trees. When they had retreated into obscurity again, he continued. "There is nothing I know of to stop such men getting us under safer control with every invention that unifies human life. They don't think of men and women, but of man-power. New methods of government help them to merge us into larger and larger flocks, to be swayed the way that suits them by words addressed to the fears of the beast. They bring about changes that seem as inevitable as a change of climate; and when they've altered the look of things, why, Mr. Travers, isn't that the natural look of things?"

"It is. But you are trying to persuade me that the power of evil is dominant."

"Evil? I didn't mention it, nor good. A gasometer is as natural as a coral reef, or it wouldn't be there. It grew out of the germs destined for gasometers."

"Yes, I suppose it did. We give body to our thoughts by using what is about us, when we've found the way. That's nothing new. It's a matter of choice. It all depends on what we want."

"That's where it is. But how many people want anything with sufficient appetite to snatch it out of the hands of luck? All they want is to be let alone. But a few men want a lot and intend to get it, and then all the means to it become their servants. The consequences are natural enough."

"I'll not deny it. I'll admit that his lordship is as inevitable as a gasometer, or the plague, or those trees across the river, if you want me to."

"Of course he is. Common opinion tends affairs that way, and it suits him. He's a leading bud in the growth of society. He's a distressing wonder, but he is as right as mastodons used to be. Give time to what he has started here, and it will change Paranagua. That forest will go. The brown Indians will become diluted till they are a dirty white. This land will look some day as if the perpetual heat of hell and some shabby palms had been added to Detroit. You and I won't be here then; but we needn't worry. The people who are here will think it is fine because it was the scene into which they were born. So what could be wrong with it? Nothing is wrong with what is familiar. It will be reality produced by the divinity of reason. We ought to glory in that. What is more, to interfere with that good work, when it really gets going and smoking, would make the guns of some government or other cock their mouths at the call of honour. Don't you think Santa Maria is a nice place for you to stay in, until the next ship—no need to look for a better?"

Travers leaned forward at the hint. It was not to see Glenthorpe more clearly; he was drawn by the pomp of the lightning in the tumult of bituminous clouds over the land beyond. The lightning was expanding in mute explosions behind summits unsuspected and dreadful, implying terrible gulfs. It was flickering in abrupt discovery along the coasts of stupendous continents in the heavens. Glenthorpe's calm profile, in one glare, more closely resembled the phosphorescent shade of a Pharaoh overlooking the casting down into oblivion of the millennia of Egypt. There were, Travers was tranquilly assured, unguessed worlds, and powers men had never called upon. But Glenthorpe suddenly moved, leaning forward, as though exasperated with his cigarette and ash-tray, and then sat back, his hands clasped behind his head.

"Now I think of it," he said, as quietly as though to himself, "the irrepressible liveliness of the human mind scares me more than the threat of earthquakes. Better not to think of it—better not to look at it. We can't do anything, but it may wreck this planet, some day."

Travers did not respond. He rose and strolled to the veranda; and Glenthorpe, still in limp repose, as if knowledge could keep no hope, and so he had subsided into indifference to whatever was to come, saw before him the back of his guest, a flimsy shape. In that twilight of celestial confusion it was no more than a diaphanous wraith of a man, an ephemeral image to be illuminated only in its moment, to last only while one of Jove's bright bolts passed through to give provisional shape to the universe. It stood uncertainly overlooking deeps where nebulæ and comets glared immensely, and were at once expunged because they were mistakes in creation; or perhaps their inscrutable and momentary purpose in it was served. The figure wavered on the rim of the globe, silent above the convulsions of light that gave glimpses of phases of eternity, as if not sure that it would remain a witness, or would vanish forever in an overbright phase. Travers faced the room, after a time, and began to pace it in composure.

"Wreck this earth, will they?" he said. "What has that to do with you or me? If they use what is at the back of that," he said, gently indicating the terror in the sky beyond, "if they use that for silly reasons, and of course they are free to do it, then it is sure to wreck them. What else would you expect? Man would not be the first creature on earth to suffer because he grew too big for his boots."

The Minister was amused. "That's it, is it? We shall go the way of the dinosaurs, when we get too big and strong for the pasture, kick up too bad a rumpus?"

"Oh, we may. I don't know. It looks like it. But the dragons never knew they were overdoing their part, nothing told them that teeth and claws were not enough. As for us, it is remarkable that we now know there is a cheat in the flesh, which rots it."

Glenthorpe frowned. He regretted to hear that, but was silent. He regretted it because he desired, for a reason he had no time then to inspect, that Travers should not prove to be gaga, after all. Glenthorpe himself never paused to speculate whether the cheat in his flesh would show itself tomorrow or a little later, for he had been watching his fellow creatures long enough to feel the less expectation of pleasing surprises. He accepted the next day quietly, when he woke up in it, and his only hope was that it would be fine and without undue hurry and noise. He could be more grateful to a good cook than to a metaphysician, and, nowadays, preferred to run a risk with the newest loudly applauded book than go to a bull-fight. It was a serious risk, but he preferred to take it; he might doze off. "The dragons," he said at length, "were no worse off for not knowing of the cheat. If they had a good time, while it lasted, it would have been damnably bad form to complain because somebody else was next for the fun."

"No, they weren't worse off for not knowing. They took the line that runs to big bellies, had what fun there was in that, and came to the end of it. They had nothing to complain about. Whatever helped dragons they got, without knowing where it would take them; and so it must be with us. But choice is here now. We know of other values. Reconciliation has come into it."

Glenthorpe had not been wholly attentive, for he had said what he had to say. He was not expecting an answer that would put out of perspective the view which satisfied him, but was musing, and was casually noting one selected purple mass of a storm which had spent its lightnings dilate slopes and terraces in a beam from the sun. The forest below was coming radiantly through. He turned his head sharply to his guest. What was he saying?

Travers saw that movement and knew his host was puzzled. A word had gone awry somewhere. "I said reconciliation, Mr. Glenthorpe. The minstrel came when the dragons went. Had you forgotten the musician?" He met Glenthorpe's inspection with ease, and was jocund in a rebuke. "Was not Psyche winged? Lives Apollo here?"

The Minister did not well disguise polite surprise. "What? What's that?" (Here it comes, he thought. Here's another of them. What a pity!)

Travers averted his face, and spoke to the landscape and clouds beyond them. "When I was young," he said, "I did what I expect you did. I made a pilgrimage to Hellas. I had to go." He made a slight gesture towards the outer scene, to the ascending ledges of nimbus in the sky, an illusion of a country removed. "But there's the kingdom, there's the right place. We want Pegasus to raise us to it, though. He can do it. I set out on foot. I knew no better. The wise man knows his own place, but the eyes of a fool are in the ends of the earth.

"You know how it is. You've been to the ends of the earth, followed by your shadow, which is all you found there worth mentioning. You looked at that, and then came back. You could have found it sooner.

"Still, the names of places, when we are young, are unreasonable, and they call us. They mean more than they tell. They're like the names of stars, which make one shudder. When we hear some places named we are awed, and secretly rejoice. Some day we will go. We think that there the world is without dust and rowdiness and noise in the peace of everlasting morning.

"You've heard that call? It's unreasonable. There's no sense in it, it has nothing to do with the guts, as though Pan were in the woods, or a cuckoo. There are sounds and names that are beyond reason. Yet what is the good of talking about that? Reasonable men and barbarians know better. They know better; they have never heard. What can be there when they don't know it? I'm talking to you."

Glenthorpe sat forward, his arms on his table, and

bent his head over a paper-knife, to inspect it, first this side of it, and then that, very carefully.

"We can only obey, when we hear," Travers murmured on, still looking at the upper slopes, "and not know why. If a call comes, cautious doubts silence it. You hear nothing, after reasonable advice has been given to you. Then you are safe again, like everybody else. I did not question it. I only went. But soon I wished I had not. I wandered about, looking for what had ceased to exist, by all the signs. So it was only a cuckoo I had heard, after all? I found nothing but archæologists and tourists, ruins, labels, and museums. The labels were correct. There is nothing wrong with our Baedekers. The facts are safe in their hands. They tell you what to look for, and it is there. Every ruin is in the right place."

(I don't think he is quite all there, surmised Glenthorpe; yet there's something in what he says.) "I know," admitted the Minister aloud. "I've been."

"I knew you had. You found, I expect, what I found. The groves are empty. I saw that with my own eyes. I was there for nothing except literature, which is worse than playing with balls when there are no gods. Hellas was relics, tourists, and sustenance for travellers provided by those who know what to sell.

I felt I was no more than a sight-seer, and that meant I had ceased to exist. I belonged to the cemetery and I was reading the interesting stones of the rest of the dead."

He paused, still watching cloudland evolving gigantic outlines in the sun. "The years it takes us to learn that it is not to be with the dead that we are called! Though what mistake could be more natural? The rich lumber of the past is the patrimony of youth, yet if he accepts it his youth goes. It is like the fatal choice in a fairy tale. He is almost certain to choose wrong, with such a heritage. What is it youth sees first but the awful outcome of the wisdom of the ages, the renowned millstones of his world, and the devotion of the influential dead to cenotaphs? And that world works. Its activities fill the land, they are the proof of human worth, and make the only noise we hear. The years that lapse, our choice made, before we learn that the light which created Hellas cannot shine there! Who would see it if it did? That bright sign is not for the dead. Only the living see it. Yet it is easier and safer to be with the dead. To leave them is a desperate adventure—to leave them and join the living in fellowship. For the world of the quick is unseen. No habitation is there, except in the heart. You may only trust it, in solitude. A time does come, though, when we know it was not for nothing that Pan was in the land before Plato, before Christ; he drew a new measure out of the void; and we follow, if we will, in the same veritable line. Did we think the pipes were lost? What, when we were played upon?" He turned and put that question to his host, who met it gravely.

"Ah, well." Travers took his chair again, and rumpled with nervous hand his greying hair, which was plentiful. The sign of cheerful resolution in eyes so innocent troubled Glenthorpe, and not altogether because he thought his understanding was better than this poor man's. He might, he judged, as well advise the wind to bear a bit more this way or that, as his guest.

"I wandered about idly," Travers told him, "enjoying the sun at least, the talk of the peasants, and the bread and wine. Because I was a student and an artist the beauty of the abandoned colonnades did not lift me up. How could I ever approach that? We lose heart for the lesser thing, when we know the greater. I remembered those stones were shaped and raised to celebrate; and what had I to celebrate, when the groves were empty, and we must listen in vain for terrible music? At last I left it. Yes, I'd had a good

155

time, but I was bringing away nothing that I had not taken there. I could have done as much in London.

"Then we were in the Gulf of Corinth, homeward bound, and I was on the bridge of the steamer with the officer of the watch. He was a saucy Londoner. In spite of the badge on his cap, and his brass buttons, his mouth and eyes were more those of a faun's than anything I had seen in Greece. He belonged to Stepney. He was very gay, when I spoke of Athens. He knew Piræus—he knew too much; but never mind that. What would you expect of a faun? Astern of us, far away, I chanced to notice a loom in the sky, a nimbus which ought not to have been there. I watched it as this merry sailor told me the latest legend of Piræus, a tale as wild and giddy as anything classical. 'What's that glow?' I asked him, and pointed astern. He swerved and peered at it seriously, as a sailor would. 'That? That's Helicon. You see its snows.'

"He was casual but certain. No doubt about this. Of course it was Helicon. This man from Stepney knew. Wouldn't a seaman know the landmarks? But did he know the effect of a dropped word? There was the summit Apollo had touched. That was the beacon I had come to see. It still burned. It was of this earth.

"That careless word! We forget it for a time. The

uproar puts it out, and we forget it. But it is there. It waits its season. It is hidden, but more potent than the needs of the day, stronger than the iron laws by which man is bound to the wheels of the vast engine he has created, wheels which are churning his lot into mud and cinders, and carrying him, he doesn't know why, God knows where. He compelled those laws, conjured the lightning out of space to harness it to his chariot, and there he is, knowing how to use it, but not what to do with it, nor how to stop it. Well, he is damned to continue his crazy course till he makes his humble surrender. Make it he must, or die. The fool, to think he could bind the sweet influences of Pleiades to any bloody purpose he chose! What does he know of those powers, except that they are submissive? Too easily harnessed! That should have made him wary. He might have guessed there was a cheat in his cleverness. If ever the heavens roll up as a scroll, it will be through Olympian laughter at us.

"For now we possess the earth, but that is all. Our desperation to make it ours has soiled its bloom. As if its bloom were without cause! And now beauty has become hateful to men,—yes, they hate it—because, I suppose, it reminds them of what they must destroy, for they have chosen darkness. It rebukes, but is silent.

They have blasted it, to make cinders. Do they know what must happen to them, if their souls turn cruel and black when they are warned that they are trying to blind God? They are lost."

Silence fell in the room. The two men did not regard each other for a spell. Santa Maria, as they saw it then, could have been the earth in a day of its original exuberance, lush with rain of genesis, when the first garden had just flowered in an arbour of a wilderness which had not found its voice; it was waiting for speech.

Travers held out his hand to it. "There is time yet. Look at that! We can always begin, and here we are. Look at that! Yet you told me we cannot do anything. We cannot choose? I've chosen! And I say the right temple has yet to be built. I say the gods come when we call. But what is it we want? And I tell you we have been soliciting in pride only for the means to greater power. What we ask for comes, when we know the right order of words, but with the gift we must take whatever is hidden in it. Our choice once was called Baal, and once its name was Barabbas. Now we give it other names, neither good nor ill, we give it many names, for the abstractions of science melt into each other, and are called fate, when our choice has decided the way material things shall go. We have learnt to conjure with the mystery that fires the constellations. We don't know what it is, but it attends our wizardry. Yes, but can we undo the work of our magic? We stand on our star and measure the universe, sure there is no hell in our successful formulas, but only the things we want. Yet we don't know, and no man to be born will ever know what is secret in the discoveries of adventuring mind, because the clue is in the last fold of ignorance.

"When will that unseal? Men have lost reverence and humility. They have lost all fear, except of each other, and in gloom watch only for the eyes of rivalry and hate, while Lucifer rises. Morning is lost on them. They have turned from it, and so fades in them the rising of praise they gave, when young, to what is lovely and of good report. They accept the hideous, and are untroubled, for that is the image of their desire. What then are the surviving tokens of their own ancient celebration of morning? Rebukes that prompt their violence. They destroy what is beautiful, foul the sky with their engines and rioting, and uncover the pit.

"What can I do, you ask? Only the one thing I can see. I will save one token still lovely from the dawn of joy, as a peace offering, and as a sign. If that goes, then another shadow must blot the earth. You tell me I shall fail—I can see that in your face. But what if I do, when I have chosen? I believe the word lives, though we all perish in the truth of it, which we do not know. I should be mad to give the lie to the light, when I see it."

Chapter Nineteen

To the bo'sun, the ritual of the entrance to dock of a British steamship, or its departure, and the fateful ceremonies along quays of northern railways, were the proprieties of a rightly ordered intelligence. They display civilization's grey and weighty purpose, which is superior to whoever serves it. Better to die than lose a boat through a faulty hitch! Bert Byles had not thought it out so far, because he had never lost gear through folly, and would have turned a sour look on any man who trifled with tackle. He did not approve of Santa Maria's railway terminus, which afflicted him as though a real thing were depraved by half-wits. There, one morning, he and Travers were. "Where's this we're off to now?" he asked.

"Zaraza, they call it."

"They would. Sounds like the name of a girl."

Bert conned his circumstances sardonically, for he had no faith in them. A minor official of this railway was smoking a cheroot, while buying fruit from an

Indian woman, who was smoking a cheroot, and whose basket was poisonous with bloated shapes in verdigris and scarlet. A superior official, who could have been an admiral but for moustaches indecorous in a seaman, loudly and dramatically supervised the purchase. A pig led the snouting of her family across the track. These people could not be trusted with a railway. Travers himself saw, though with enjoyment, that the station suggested that the people gracefully lolling here had been having a game, and now were resting. They had become tired of it, and had just dropped it. They were not going to play at trains any more that day. He and Bert were too late to join in; they might as well go away. But a locomotive continued to amuse itself, at a little distance. It wore a funnel like a carnival hat, and was larking with some trucks, bumping the protesting things boisterously, and shrieking at every recoil. Nobody gave it any attention. You could see they were used to its frolics; they knew that healthy young engine. Only an audience of tall palms bent their heads above this game called shunting, looking on. Beyond the palms, showing through as extravagantly disordered shrubbery, were the walls of houses so ardently coloured and suggestively ambushed that Travers supposed they had been left behind when a cinema photographer had departed, having no further use for his arrangement of a setting for high romance.

"I'd like to know," said the bo'sun, "what's going to happen at—at this place you spoke of. If we get there."

"So would I. We'll go there and see."

"Ah. Same here. Did that consul tell you anything? What did he say about the *Cairngorm*? Anything?"

"No, Bert. Nothing for certain. He didn't know."

"Didn't he, though? He's the sort of consul. Well, it's time he was told. I met her steward, and she's not here for bananas."

"Isn't she? She could have plenty if she wanted them."

The bo'sun peered round tactfully for the proof of happiness in his companion, who showed it, for the rhetoric of the station admiral when persuading the pigs to depart was attractive, and at the same time he was remembering the ironic humour of Glenthorpe when he left him. "For all you know," said the Minister, "I may be an agent for his lordship." Glenthorpe, he decided, was a great swell. He was glad he had met Glenthorpe.

A squad of soldiers shambled noisily into the station. They made themselves at ease. They were disrespectful to their rifles, and crouched and sprawled, while smoking. An officer, in a uniform of pale blue, with silver braid, whose babyish face was wistful with a sneer grained by sickness into its lemon complexion, allowed one of his men to light a cigarette at his own.

Byles did not miss that. These troops were as inappropriate as the railway station, and the pigs had come back. The locomotive continued to shriek deliriously in its lonely capers. An hour after it was due to depart the train backed in. The pigs and chickens gave way to it indolently. Its parts were promiscuously assembled, but most of its length was box cars. Very conspicuously it had one Pullman coach; and also an American engine driver, whose demeanour, as he took stock of the crowd, and then lowered himself from his cab, told the bo'sun that a deliberate man was present. The seaman was surprised to find there the stamp of a peremptory male; and after satisfying his sense of the good with the autocratic bearing of this engine-driver, who was then telling the admiral what to do with himself, Bert went along to the locomotive, homesick for an exchange of technical and allusive English.

A bell tolled. The troops scaled the box-cars in

haste. The weekly train was off; and it might, so judged the passengers in the Pullman, reach Zaraza that night; though perhaps not, for it was as well to remember that it was a temperamental line, and sometimes ran away with a flood.

No. The soldiers were not going with them because trouble was expected. They were to guard the mines. A young English surveyor became mirthful—he had the joy of knowing dismal news hidden from the innocent. He told the other fellows in the Pullman not to kid themselves; he had met a man; and the soldiers might have to shoot; what about a spot of excitement for a rotten trip? Take it from him. He hoped, in gaiety, that they would reach the mines with insides all complete.

Now they were out of Santa Maria, running between the walls of a forest, which came so close that leaves brushed them, where trees had fallen. It looked as though they were the last train to pass through before the jungle closed over the track. A party of monkeys fled howling, hurried by shots and shouts loosed from the box-cars. The shots broke speech from Bert. Soldiers like them, he grumbled, would be about as useful as penny squirts at a fire. Fighting monkeys, though; ah, only give 'em monkeys! But, answered the bass of a German, at mutilations they are too good. Dead mens, yes. They are good at dead mens. I have seen. It is very bad.

The foliage fleeting alongside slowed down, and crawled past. It stopped, and a pendant tangle of vines stood opposite the conversations for so long that it became familiar. It was reflected in a pool. The young English surveyor said that bit of the track was tricky, every now and then it wasn't there; once he shot a tiger drinking at that pool; it sat too long surprised by the train; funny thing, I nearly looked too long at the tiger, but woke up first. Got him! Bit of luck, but just then the train moved on.

It moved on again. Anybody ring? The steward, a negro, whose brow was grey, stood melancholy at respectful attention. We all rang, uncle! Every finger pressed the button! The surveyor was facetious with the old negro, who smiled as if at a jest somewhat bitter, but with the tolerance of age in attendance on light-hearted youth. What'll you have? The train was speeding through a bare upland country of rocks and low bushes as shapeless as squatting beasts. The forest had retired to the background. It would make a feint of running down to crowd the track again, and then would glide away to a greater distance.

The speed of the train surprised the passengers. Now she's doing it. Got a nerve, that engine-driver! Shouldn't care to chance it myself, not on this track. She's steeple-chasing. She'll loop the loop. Good man, that. Bert supposed the driver didn't know whether he'd get through. Trying to make it, Bert expected. Why not get through? Why should he, if he's ditched? What did he tell me? He said it was asking for it to carry troops to the mines.

Oh, come off! You can get that stuff in Paranagua whenever you listen. Use it in your bath. We've heard it before. It's all the same as gin at the Anglo-American Club. It's like the great new oil-field. When it's found, don't believe it, till you're there. Where's that porter? Isn't there any ice? What'll you have?

The rhythm of the train was comforting. It was soothingly confident of continuance. Travers, watching the land, heard only fragments of the conversation, which was desultory. Have you seen that Polish woman at the Hotel La Paz? No. Only heard about her. You don't catch Glenthorpe. He's a hidalgo. He's close. Not sure that I like him—I fancy he's laughing at us. You know what I mean. What I say is, leave the birds alone; the price of rubber won't go up, will it? A country like this, left to the spiders and flies. Too bad, to let people run it who won't do anything with it, and skin us if we try.

Travers could see nothing in the land to make trouble. Nobody was there. At times it was forest, with huge leaves like fingers flung so close to his face that he flinched from his lookout; it was startling when the land almost touched him, for then it was real. It retreated obliquely and swiftly into a transient phantasy that passed with his own hours. A glass smashed. He took instant stock of the tumblers on the table. They stood there as before. The German opposite was staring at the landscape, open-mouthed.

Travers turned to see, and horsemen were going headlong on the skyline. Another window crashed. A rough scar flicked across the mahogany over the German's head; but Travers' interest was jerked from that prodigy when the train leaped immediately with greater speed. That winded him against the table. The big German was struggling to get away from the window, his spectacles swinging from one ear. The coach began to rock and bump. Bert embraced Travers, lifted him clear into the central alleyway, and lay on him. "Still, guv'nor. She's off the line."

The pounding and splintering abruptly ceased. The coach began slowly to tilt sideways. It changed its mind and dropped back squarely, as though too tired to do more. Travers was numbed, but could hear Bert breathing in his ear, and then began the buzzing roar of steam escaping. The locomotive was dying; he could hear that, so he supposed he must be present. Bert carefully rose. "You keep where you are, mister." He put a kindly foot on Mr. Travers. "Wait a minute." Travers, however, wouldn't have it, and pushed it off.

But he could see nothing outside except the blaze of the sun on an empty slope of tumbled rocks and bushes, which were knocking and slamming. A woman was screaming. The wire spring of a berth twanged like a harp, and dust puffed from it. "A bit this way, mister; keep lower."

The negro steward came up and stood near them, mourning. The gashed mahogany and the torn upholstery had upset him. "O Lordy, look, who pay fer dis?" A window blind lazily burned; it spun and fluttered when another bullet tore through it. Travers decided to douse it, but was staggered by the negro, who pitched against him, and then slid down on his back, too heavy for Travers to hold, staring in astonished enquiry at the roof of the coach, while the brown of his face turned to lead. Travers knelt to the negro, whose limp hand had ceased to twitch. "Foul," he exclaimed.

"What's that, mister?" asked Bert. "Ah," he muttered, glancing downwards, "poor old uncle's got it. I thought it was dangerous.

"Mind the other side, Mr. Travers. They're firing both sides. They've got us cooked."

The train, like the upland rocks on each side, was thumping and banging. Men were beneath the floor of the coach, firing from the track. Three soldiers came stooping along the passage of the Pullman, and began sniping from the windows. One of them, a grinning boy, asked Bert for a cigarette. He appeared to be rapt, Travers noticed, in this game with a rifle, and smoked, and grinned eagerly, and deftly worked the bolt of his gun, shooting at a hillside. In the midst of his enjoyment his rifle clattered to the floor, and he went to sleep, snoring loudly face downwards on a seat, and the back of his head had gone. Bert shouted, dived for the rifle, and had it at the window in a moment, sternly watching those rocks. Travers went to him, took the rifle from his friend, and dropped it outside. "That's enough."

"But by God they want to kill us!"

"They don't know what they're doing. It's ugly work, not yours. It's madness. Keep still."

"Dammit, mister, have we got to die because they're mad and we're not?"

"Very likely."

A woman continued to screech steadily, and mechanically. That was more noticeable, because the banging from the train had almost ceased. Scattered groups of men appeared on the hills and were trailing down stealthily towards them. The officer in blue was very conspicuously outside, a revolver in his hand, shouting an order, sneering and dignified. Nobody answered. He was alone. He was shouting sternly again when he tottered; his authoritative voice slurred away into a murmur, and he dropped.

Chapter Twenty

BERT'S EYEBROWS LIFTED. HE SHOOK HIS HEAD. "THAT kid asked for it. Shouldn't have thought he had it in him." The bo'sun plunged at his pockets and brought out his pipe and a hairy skin pouch, and fumbled them, for they were diminished in his big deliberate paws. "That young un, he was the goods, . . . may as well have half-a-dozen draws before the bump. Here come the swine." He wondered how Travers was taking it. His own hate went bloody when he heard the taunts bawled in triumph outside, and saw Travers waiting as if he were merely tired and wished this row would stop. Didn't he know? Travers met his anxious solicitude, and smiled.

They watched a soldier run out towards a body of horsemen, crying distractedly and waving his hands above his head. One of the riders bent over and shot him. "See that? If I had a gun," growled Bert. Travers was silent, and his eyes were closed. Then he roused and touched Bert's hand, which was gripping a table. "Don't fuss. You can't resist this. It isn't worth it."

172

Insolence, nervous but bustling, presently discovered them, and covered them with its rifles. They were ordered out; and Travers held up his hands loosely in a surrender displeasing to a victor, who poked a gun barrel into his back with force. Bert cried "Hey there," and swerved dangerously, but he was told to act as he was bidden. The passengers were lined up by the dead officer, whose exquisite sneer upturned before them was firm even under the crawling of flies. A wounded man raised himself rigidly by the track stressed by pain, but went limp under a passing swipe from a machete. The rebels were happy and boisterous as they swarmed in their looting of the wrecked train. Bert's frowning interest became still more severe when a youth went through his pockets, as if a dummy must be harmless, spilled a few articles on the ground as valueless, smelt the tobacco and sneezed, tried the pipe, though with no pleasure, and crumpled in brisk contempt a letter or two. The sweating passengers stood meekly in the heat, uncertain whether an impatient gesture in their dislike of flies, which swarmed, would be misunderstood, for they could see what caprice, now jocular in victory, could do with mortality. "Have you seen my spectacles?" asked the German of Travers. "I haf lost my spectacles. What must happen to us? I cannot see."

Nobody could see. Some leaders of the rebels sauntered that way, and reviewed the prisoners in intent animosity and perplexity. They questioned them, and listened to what they were told in sour disbelief. They debated the fate of these people. To execute them, so the subjects of the discussion could hear, for the argument was vigorous, might not be useful; yet again, if they were spies? Beyond doubt they were a nuisance, for whom there was no transport, and no place for internment. What then? The rebel guard languidly nursed its weapons, and waited in indifference to do whatever it was ordered to do.

The officers, while still grouped by the sense of duty, uncertain of the right thing to do, paused to listen to a sentry, who drew their attention to the distance. Two horsemen had appeared on the skyline, and one seemed to be signalling. That apparition was watched with a vigilance which presently lessened the activity about the train. Captors and captured became united in a gaping expectancy. Prisoners were forgotten. The train was forgotten; chance once more had veered the purpose of mortals, as a fickle puff gives direction to thistledown. A whistle sounded, and the victors scattered to another and an unseen task.

Bert plucked at Travers, and edged him prudently towards the head of the train. The locomotive was lying, its wheels uppermost, the earth around ploughed up by its last struggles, on the far side of a low embankment. The body of the driver had tumbled within the shadow under the lee of it. But they found the driver was not so dead, or so sound asleep, as he appeared to be, when whispered to confidingly in English. He opened his eyes and turned his head. He exclaimed irreverently. He had been resting, fairly comfortable, but not hopeful, in the poor expectation that his body would be of no interest. "Say, is our luck coming back?" he asked Bert. "Better help it along. Keep your face out of sight."

Chapter Twenty-one

THE THREE MEN SHELTERING BY THE LOCOMOTIVE listened to spasmodic rifle fire, but could see only a staring desert, which was unnaturally still and empty, for it thudded and rattled. The crepitation dwindled to a fitful tapping, and ceased. Then they could hear the flies. They helped to maintain this hush, fearing to move, feeling that a jolt might upset peace into a senseless racket again.

The engineer gazed heavenward quizzically. A loose cluster of black dots was drifting in the vault, like fragments of burnt paper circling in a slow vortex of the upper air. "They're being kept from their grub," he remarked.

"Grub," questioned the bo'sun, "which?"

The engineer nodded to the sky. "Them—the vultures."

The firing burst out again in a galloping delirium. The engineer laughed. Hell, still at it! The bo'sun's eyes were upturned to the black specks circling remotely. Now he knew what they had to do with him. What time would they come down to their grub? Since the three men began to wait Travers had not spoken nor stirred. He sat with his back against the boiler lost in the contemplation of the butterflies which danced in a life apart about a shrub in flower, beside which lay the crumpled funnel of the engine.

The boiler rang sharply at a blow, and a sibilant singing followed it, as if a tenuous steam-pipe had been cut, and it still held some flowing energy. The engineer half-turned to listen. "Sounds as if she's in song again. No. She's too full of holes. She's bust. That's a cicada. Damlot he cares." The metal clanged again under a double knock, and a ricochet mounted in a long whine over their heads. "I thought," complained Bert, "I'd heard the last of that dirty noise some years ago. Can they see us?"

"That'u'd be all right if they could see us," the engineer assured him. "It's the guys that can't see us worries me—them fellers never know what they'll hit. I got one of them, though," he chuckled. "I got him. He stood on the track and waved his arms. Tried to fascinate me, I guess. But she was still on the track. These greasers take time to think and he didn't get enough."

Several spurts of dust were instantaneous by the shrub, but they did not interrupt the pulsing of the butterflies. The frantic but unseen hammers continued to tap the horizon rapidly, using it as the rim of an inordinate coffin for men, which must be closed before dark; yet the cicada near the three men in hiding, who were hoping they would be left out, that the hammering would not enclose them, continued to whisper its song as though the shadow of the first doubt had still to fall on earth, and darkness was unknown.

"Anyway, I got one of them." The engineer repeated his satisfaction. "I got him." The vultures remained as black specks in the vault, and Travers watched a radiant bubble of emerald floating about the shrub before him, a humming bird evasive as a gleam in a crystal. The atom poised, with wing-beats an aureola, before a white pendulous blossom, and agitated it, and then vanished as though the air flawed. It was joyous and free. There was a world in which that aerial creature lived, and not the impact of engines in disastrous anarchy, nor all the bullets, could penetrate it. It was inviolable. Travers saw that men could move about in that world to destroy each other, yet could not enter it, for they did not know they could have it.

The hammering became intermittent toward sunset. Its fury waned. The engineer was hopeful. "Give me a shadow long enough to crawl on, and I'll get some grub before them birds. What's the time? Sunset in twenty minutes! We'll make it yet." He spat for luck.

The engineer presently stooped away out of it. "Wait right here," he told the other two. "One's enough. I guess I can dig out the stuff."

It was night when he returned. "Now we're on it. Bite into this. Can't say how you fellers feel about it, but I want a drink. You could strike matches on my tongue. Here we are . . . how's that? Anybody there, says you? Well, I ask you! Am I whispering? No, there's only lots of stiffs lying around. I noticed they plugged that bright young guy, that friend of yours, that Englishman. He was going to Zaraza to sink a well or open a canteen. I fell over him. He didn't say anything. Let's have some eats."

"What'll we do now?" asked Bert.

"Do? Didn't I say eat? After that I'll show you." Bert knew a leader when he met him. This job wasn't seamanship, and if Mr. Travers was to be steered clear of folly in a place where you couldn't tell reefs from deep water, this American was the man for his money. Bert was mollified by the engineer's nonchalant skill with awkward facts. Always back the man who knows the ropes.

The engineer fed himself rapidly and talked. "They've bust their line, they've capsized their country to settle who'll have the right to rob it, and now they're carrion for the buzzards and bugs. All we want now is small-pox. I knew something was going to breeze along when that swell lord was at Zaraza a month ago. By name of Snarge. You heard of him? He's this track and the mines and all, so they say. He spoke to me in the cab one day, and I tell you I wouldn't like to put poison in that gangster's soup, for if he told me he didn't see me do it I wouldn't believe him. Do I blame him? Like hell I don't. He wouldn't worry about a little annoyance like this. When he rattles the dice he knows it's three sixes for him every time. Did you say was he up there now? Now, would you hang around after the gang had got its dope? When the boys light out to fetch the stuff you go home to wait for it."

"So you don't blame him?" asked Travers.

"Sure I don't. I don't blame buzzards. They know

their meat. I can see better rolling stock and a real track coming out of this. It's been a one-horse show too long. There's no taste in good pay if the job makes you feel like a museum doorman on a Sunday. What we'd better do is to climb out of this. If we loose this chance, I'd blush to look a high-pressure gauge in the face again."

Travers was in no hurry to move, not while night was closely seamed with the glimmering tracks of interlacing fireflies. He knew what had happened—as a capsule ripened in the firmament the moon had burst. Its fallen molecules were wandering in search of good ground driven by the need of their primary essence to illuminate the dark. Now they could only quicken it with diamonds; they would disperse it presently. The other two men shaped faintly when several glowing blobs swerved near them. The night was warm and fecund. Seeds of light were being sown broadcast. He had no desire to leave that corner, where he was assured of generation within the lower darkness of earth by an abundance of star grain; but he rose to go—he had no misgiving; and he confided in this stranger, who said only what was in him, and honestly admitted without complaint that things were as he saw them.

He and Bert followed the engineer, whose promptitude betrayed purpose; and the bo'sun was wary, keeping his chief in touch, though conscious of the silent and imminent unknown at his own back. He cursed those fireflies. They were foolishness. The darkness swam with them, as if it was drunk. How could that fellow ahead keep a course when there were thousands of binnacle lamps all loose and doing different ways? Steering a craft with a compass like a teetotum! The bo'sun had never thought he would look back on a middle watch of those distant years when submarines were about and think it was a good time. He should have stuck to ships. A ship at sea is the only right place when the world is blotto.

They stumbled over the railway track, and soon were feeling their way downhill. The night was thicker at the bottom of the slope, and without even a firefly. They could smell rank mould and wet and rotting leaves. The bo'sun, though he couldn't make out anything, had a desire to keep his hands before his face, to fend things off.

The engineer paused to light his pipe. He did it at irreverent leisure. His match showed, for a few moments, that they were watched by a crowd of sinuous tree-trunks and boughs, which apparently had been confused in a noiseless riot till the unexpected spurt fixed the tumult in its last contortions. The refugees were on a path, and when the engineer halted later, and spoke, his voice was hollow, and was returned in echoes, as from an enclosing vault. "There's a boat here," he said, surprisingly. "There's no greaser near it—not in this place—they wouldn't come here on a bet."

He made another light to show them. The trees were still there, but not on earth. They rose as piers from a polished black floor, for the forest was under water, and they supported midnight. There was no movement and no sound. There was a boat by a miniature jetty. The scene wavered when the light faded, as if it depended on their astonished eyes; then it closed in and vanished.

Chapter Twenty-two

THE BO'SUN GRIPPED A PADDLE, AS A LAST STRAW. IT was doing something he knew. Its nice balance and the smooth texture of its handle satisfied him with an illusion of the familiar. So did the uncertainty of his foothold as they embarked, though they had to feel their way into the boat. His mind was at home when his feet moved for compensation on a rocking floor. He was in a hurry to get safe water behind him, but remembered that his last view was of trees ahead. Trees! He was humbled. "How do we go?" he asked.

"Hold on there, sailor. It's deep. I got a lantern—darn the thing I can't fix it. Are you going to steer a boat over tree-tops that ain't there? I'll have it in a minute."

While they waited they heard the energetic engineer breathing heavily as he fiddled with tinware in the bows. He became impatient and swore, and relinquished the obstinate thing for a spell. "Time in plenty," he told himself.

In that brief pause Travers was surprised that whatever was about them could be both blind and dumb. Yes, the water was at hand; he could touch it. It was tepid. Time in plenty! They seemed to be where nothing had happened to set time going, and that, of course, made an engineer impatient to begin it; that man wanted to start time ticking along with the sounds of progress.

The bo'sun, however, was suspecting already that he might be alone and abandoned, that he had been left behind in last week—hey, where's that lantern?—when there was a monstrous plunge near them.

The boat rocked. Echoes fled lugubriously and fearful. "Some alligator, that" supposed a diffident voice, to end a suspense. They heard the fumbling begin hurriedly, and then a glint was held aloft. The man in the bows stared around. Nothing was there but traces of melting gold on the disquieted black flood.

They sidled away into the deep of it. The engineer, relieved that one more trifling obstruction was past, began to bawl a ribald song now the boat had way on her. "Sailor, don't go after the birds." Bert was deft but anxious; he had this to do, and expertly twisted his craft about threats suddenly present and barely glimpsed. It seemed to him that a loud voice was bad there, anyhow—it multiplied into a rowdy crew in that deep hole. This song about birds was indecent; singing that stuff in the grave! Water was all around, yet full of trees, which grew up while he wasn't looking. That guiding lantern was only a matchflare in a place capsized off common-sense. Birds! Was it a boat or a balloon? The fairway was no better than a lucky patch spread by the lantern. The water followed them about.

"A bit more to your left, sailor, there's garden right ahead." The engineer held the lamp aloft.

The steerman saw pale objects drift towards them in a dreamy procession. He ducked from tentacles abruptly lowered on them by the lamp. Nothing had touched them yet; this wasn't right; to the bo'sun it was the same as hoping to dodge all the queer things in a bad dream, and trying to wake up.

But the engineer remembered other ditties, at intervals. He chanted fragments of them to the echoes. He was alert and light-hearted. He made improper comparisons, as grisly shapes went past. He asked Travers how he liked it.

Travers answered modestly. To him the interlude was not unrelated, for he had been in great cities after dark, and he understood them as well as he did the shades about him then. This river, or whatever it was, might be Acheron of the lower world, to which everybody came, but not the sun. The piers and the stalactitic shapes were what supported a morning floor for the living; and there, perhaps, was the opening through which people descended to the lower place. He thought he could discern ahead a thinning of the gloom, as by starlight at the end of a tunnel.

The boat touched; they had come to earth. The air had a flow, and they could see through it to the stars. Their guide made fast the boat, and led a climb up an escarpment, which needed no lantern, to a level where they found the end of a street of small houses. Under the quiet sky, and in that kindling air, the pale walls glowed nebulously as with bluish moontide absorbed from the last phase and not yet all radiated. In the walls were splashes and hollows of bright lemon. They could hear music at the far end of the village.

The engineer stopped when he reached the music, which was the drone of a gramophone, and listened and grinned. He thumped on the door with authority. It was opened to a cautious chink and merely an eye, but when the engineer greeted the eye frivolously the door was flung wide in welcome by a large and unctuous man, neither Indian nor white, who stood and wabbled his head solemnly and made noises in his throat of loving surprise. Then he embraced the engineer, while murmuring words of endearment. The round and ample host turned to the company within, and announced the newcomers impressively. His introduction had the grand manner, to show that these new guests were his intimates and of royal rank. The engineer stepped into the room boldly, and the bo'sun followed him in no doubt, for he thought he had sniffed such a house before, somewhere or other, no matter where. Travers entered because there was nothing else to do.

The company stood in the last turn of its dance, uncertain of the nature of the interruption. The gramophone went on. There were a number of girls, and the nearest of them showed they remembered the engineer, though their admission was faint, perhaps because of indifference, or because other men were near. Yet he knew he was at home, Travers could see. The women who were deeper in the shadows, or whose tincture was nearer chocolate than jaundice, had eyes and teeth as distinct as their frocks of white cotton. The newcomers were watched in sullen dislike by some of the men, but these were barefooted and meagre fellows, and would not be noticed by a confident engineer who had to bow his head when he passed under the oil-lamp hanging from the centre of the ceiling, unless he gave them some attention, and he didn't give them any.

The hostel was roomy, and its floor of earth was smooth as pitch through age and use. Its extent would have been random with that sooty lamp, but for the bare chalky walls, of whitewashed mud, which displayed the black heads and brown masks in relief.

Travers fancied they were simple peons, much nearer the Children of the Sun than the Conquistadores, though there was some infection of the greensickness of Europe. They had that saintly look of wan renunciation to patronage. They were devout—they had turned from worship of the Sun to the bead-roll. Near him on the wall was a picture of the Virgin. He snuffed a pervasive odour of herbs, the lamp, musk, and bodies, and what arose from the seepings in the old floor. The smell was more foreign to his mind than the darkest Indian rites. His nose made him shudder a little, and the room was close. There was no way out of it. There was more of horror in that incense and heat than in the blank depths of the night sky. It might be the proof of original sin, if that had a smell.

Then he was cheered. Unaware, his attention caught on a figure. A girl stood beneath the picture, and with her ivory pallor and dark demure eyes, and the tender vacancy of her face, she could have been its subject, except that she had a red flower in her hair. She was alone. What was that image of innocence doing there?

The host was still lifting his shoulders, and spreading his hands, in mock woe—ah! these ingrates, these rebels, dogs!—gesturing fancifully to the engineer, an affable and bawdy showman, dabbing a small pink handkerchief at his forehead, and wagging a finger at his nose. Wait! He reproved himself. Come with him! He loftily conducted his three guests to a kitchen. They must be famished. They must be fed in a befitting manner.

A negress fed them, a woman of tonnage in a turban, who was happy because affairs were all buoyant with fun, and that made her pause, while serving them, to shake with boneless mirth. The engineer and the bo'sun gave her plenty of nonsense in return, which she broadened. She noticed in soft alarm that Travers was silent, and seemed not to be hungry. She was solicitous and motherly, bending to him her bosom of a full brood. He must have fever. He was English, she told him. So was she, she assured him kindly. With her he was safe. She was English. She came from Jamaica.

When they rejoined the dancers they were unseen. The measure had full control, and the men and women had no eyes but for themselves. They bent to each other invitingly, making signs. Their hands clapped to a rhythm which could not be broken. The measure was deliberate and mesmeric, with occasional emphasis and a cry. Some of the men had swung themselves free. They quickened the more sluggish. Their flourishes were generous. The earth agreed with the pulsation of their feet. Travers felt, for his own resting body answered the tremor of the earth, that this movement must be prompted from the centre; the dance was a ritual answering a blind compulsion. The bo'sun and the engineer were drawn into it, and the sailor's stout efforts soon flowed easily with the common zeal which shook the floor and made the room hot and acrid. A youngster stamped and whirled beside Travers, not seeing him, her eyes fixed, and breathing quickly in sighs through her lips parted in transport.

Travers began to find it as dreary as watching a

spinning wheel. He edged by the wall, away from it. He had lost sight of Bert. He escaped into another apartment, and there he found the bo'sun, with the girl who so much resembled the subject of the sacred picture. She was submissive and languorous. The flower had gone from her hair. The sailor had it behind his ear.

Chapter Twenty-three

TRAVERS BACKED OUT WITHOUT DISTURBING THEIR
pleasure. The unlighted passage through which too
briskly he groped his way was inconsiderate with
sharp turns. He eased up. There was no need for
flight. His instinctive politeness tickled him. As if a
pair so busy would have noticed him! And you can't
embarrass old Priapus. The way surprised eyebrows lift
at his antics only adds to his happiness. It is part of the
fun.

Still, on reflection, Travers hoped his own instinctive and mannerly retreat was as natural as any behaviour of the bacchantes. There was something to be
said for it. Though certainly he was rather like a fish
on a hearth-rug, the fact that he was there made him
as native to the landscape as the house itself, the
corpses on the railway track, and the alligator swamp.
Certainly the house had surprised him—he had forgotten Zaraza could not be so very far away, a mining
place, a hive of industry always short of balm; once

more he was left to wonder where to find his place in the common lot.

This dark passage he was in, whither did it lead? He found his own melancholy fun in a conjecture that he sought a sanctuary which had no existence. Life has no use for sanctuaries, and does not provide them. Something must be wrong with him, he doubted, some obstruction of the rosy juices, some closure by fastidiousness—which could make a man as inert as the ivory figure of a crucifix—when he could no more accept the stream of life as it was going, plunge into it amid the promiscuous flotsam and jetsam, like the rest of hearty men, than mock the altars of the devout.

Life was gross and wasteful, of course, so cruelty was as usual as merriment. If it were not gross it would not be here. The waste issued from its very profusion. If the first man had been an artist, then he might also have been the last man. The stream would have failed at its source, and Eve would have sighed as she tended the animals. No barbarians; but no Apollo. The flow must carry all on its tide, garbage and stuff gone to waste, Cleopatra's barge, and the cradle of Moses. You must take the lot. But he was as separate in that house—he regretted his aversion, somehow—as he was in the fight in the train. He could only turn from the odour of it, which was as pronounced as that of a fragrant lily; and turn on the instant, too. All he could do in a fight was to stand and be shot at. There was no alternative that he could see. If life went that way, then he must go another.

He stumbled into something, and a dog's yelp ended that speculation. His consoling words brought only a snarl from the dark. An urgent scramble of the animal abruptly ended. He found it had fled through an opening in the wall, and he followed it; and in a breath, standing upright, had the large and impersonal dark to himself.

This was more like home. His imprisoned antipathy left him, as though rankling doubts were absorbed at once into the universal, and were lost, just as the sea takes in all, and is the same. He could see about him a few low hummocks that were buildings, but could have passed as outcrops of rock. That stratum of shadow beyond must be the forest of the prime. But that could do nothing to embarrass him; he expected nothing from it. Night in this unknown and unseen wilderness had the familiarity of a private thought. He was its intimate. It could not surprise him. The sky drew from him the dubiety and distraction that came of rubbing shoulders in a crowd, and ac-

cepted him in solitude. He could laugh now at that
rascal the showman, who was of no more consequence under the stars than the yelp of the dog. He
could remember here that the silent universe included
Bert's fidelity—that was present, too—and the insouci-
ance of the engineer who took the ruin of his train and
pretty ladies in the day's work; and the sagacity and
kindness of Glenthorpe; virtues as right as the planets.
What light he had, where nothing much was clear,
was as authentic, if as distant and tremulous, as was
that of the Pleiades. Why pray to learn to what it
would lead? There is no need to worry over the re-
motest and more delicate of the glims. They are well
set. There they are, not without cause.

He found his way down to the river, drawn by the
murmur of it, the only sound in the night. Its current
was no more than an undertone, as though he heard
darkness running out; he could hear the gloom of the
primitive jungle being drained in volume continuously
from the earth. He could wait—wait till all had gone.
Nor was he without kin. That dog had followed him,
and at a respectful distance was patient. It came closer,
when invited, and stretched for sleep. He looked, after
long, to see whether the height of the forest athwart
the sky had been lowered by the outflowing murk.

It seemed no less. That lessening takes time; but he knew that some of it must have gone.

When next he roused, morning had touched the roof of the forest across the stream. The cornice of fronds and sprays was spreading in flames. Now that day had come, who could imagine there had been chaos? Stones began tumbling above him, and he turned. There stood the bo'sun, at a pause in his hurry, his frowning alarm just softening into relief.

Bert mumbled, and was shy. "All alone here? Been by yourself, eh?" He noted with disapproval the rocks, the weighty torrent, and the tangle, savage and towering, on its opposite shore.

"No, I've not been alone."

The bo'sun glanced at the drooping mongrel sitting near, and then in questioning disbelief at Travers. Not alone? That dog? What was the guv'nor getting at now? But Mr. Travers seemed happy, as though he knew of a good joke.

Chapter Twenty-four

If all the way to paranagua, wherever that was, were to be as good as this, then Bedlam itself must have its sunny hours. Mrs. Travers noticed preparations to lower the ship's gangway, leaning on the rail. The ship was moving on, but only when you looked down to the water unwinding along its side. The sea went in coils astern without breaking. The men were not hurrying. The water was noiseless. To break the glass of the sea, to upset the poise of such a morning, would be as clumsy as dropping good luck, even when you didn't quite know where to put it.

Where are we now? Oh, the Bahamas! Yes, the Bahamas! She'd forgotten them. Were they the same as the Bermoothes? The steward didn't know; he'd never heard of them. We shan't be here long, miss, but there's a shore party.

In a real ship with tourists and cocktails you soon learn there are shore parties for Nombre de Dios, Lesbos, Valhalla, and Laputa, and you are never surprised.

The steward warns you in good time. Madam, we shall be at the City of the True Cross for two hours. Shall I put up some sandwiches for you? Ham?

No, she didn't think she would go ashore. She watched a tangle of amber-coloured weed drift by in water of so clear a blue that it was her own fault if she could not see deeper into it. A thought had to be simple and direct to penetrate into that bottomless serenity. She felt too lazy to do it, too. She'd been doing too much thinking, and you can never see very far after doing that.

Was that an island they had come to, or was it only the captain's imagination? It must be an island. The old captain never imagined things, except when he was looking far too artful at dinner, making his crow's-feet very noticeable, telling them about passengers he had never met, on voyages long ago.

The Bahamas! This might be the very island on which Columbus landed. But its shore glittered as if it were new that morning. Its luminous stalk of a lighthouse could never want a lantern. But that land barely existed. It was a miracle that its faint green and gold persisted almost level with the ocean under the glare of all the sky. She tried to see it as Columbus saw it.

This, too, was the first time; it is alway the first time for somebody.

She supposed, a moment ago, that she was really feeling as Columbus did when he gazed at the happy confirmation, on the day when the veritable sea was breaking on his dream. There it was. There actually it was, and nobody but himself had had the faith. The world had come right way up and exhilarating when he was almost ready to admit there was no hope in it. She had felt as good as Columbus till those two girls came laughing round the other end of the deck. The same two. They had been very entertaining to Mantell and the Doctor last night. That one with the prim hair neatly parted over her forehead like black enamel on a draper's idol would have changed the opinion of Columbus about any island; San Salvador was not the name he would have called it, if she had interrupted his meditation.

No. Perhaps this wasn't the first of the Americas; this wasn't his island. It was her island. In gratitude she would call it San Salvador. John Travers, you can't escape from me this time; that friend of Mantell's, the Minister at Santa Maria, was sure they could find him before he left the country. So no shore party for her. The island was better as she saw it then. The dream must be kept. You can never tell on what triviality a dream will go to pieces if you land on it with a shore party.

Santa Maria, Paranagua; what names! They had been taken, she expected, from a luscious book. Yet what could John be doing in that legendary country? She had never heard him even mention it. There could be only one reason for his being there—no reason—no reason at all. That gave her a voyage which was even harder than was the discovery of America to Columbus. How does one overtake a shadow which is thrown from nothing? Or catch one of those ghost candles they saw up aloft in the ship's rigging the other night—what were they called? Yes, how does one catch a Corpo Santo?

Down went the anchor. Now everything was balanced and complacent. Only that mirror of an island continued to flicker, and she listened for the sound of it, but the silence was one with the sky. Perhaps those people ashore—if such a shore had any people— thought this was the usual phantom ship. They were used to strange mirages in the distance. They had never heard of shore parties. Very likely ships had appeared offshore here before, perhaps once or twice in a lifetime, and nobody on the island ever knew why. A ship arrived just as a small cloud floats along from nowhere in particular and makes no difference. The Spanish Main, she could see, was of the morning that has no beginning and cannot end. It was eternal day without an after-lunch. Not even buccaneers could break into this sea. As for their own ship, a landing party was silly. Ships and men in that splendour could have no more effect than noisy voices. When everybody had stopped talking there wouldn't be so much as a ripple left in the air.

The best thing about being in a ship, she considered, is that it is foolish to question anything. Probably a thing is there, if you see it, even an island. It was a holiday from curiosity. You didn't know anything, and to ask questions was simply to show your awful ignorance. Nobody expected you to help. Even Mrs. Grundy dared not meddle; she had to look on and tremble with envy. If there were any laws they were the laws of the sea and you didn't know them. The sun came up, but it was the same day, and night fell, but only to show it was time to dance. You forgot when you embarked, and forgot the voyage would end. It was a suspension in limbo, with some nice people, and some others. Only a scrap of sharp memory interrupted now and then, like the sudden dip of a sea-bird, a lively atom quite distinctly separate, to remind you that you had not really escaped; that the old life went on, and was drawing you imperceptibly yet with inescapable influence through what was the calm apparition of another existence.

Anyhow, there that apparition was, while it lasted, and when you stared at it long enough it was as satisfying as the truth, bright, bare, immense, and inexplicable, making you feel very small, yet giving you quiet. What was so vast must be inexplicable. Why, there was nothing but your tiny and wondering soul to look on, and how could the truth hurt anything so insignificant? A pity John had not seen things that way; then—why, then she wouldn't have been there; and how much she would have missed!

There was nothing of the phantom about the Captain, all the same. There he came, tumbling accurately down the steep ladder from his bridge—never any women up there, she heard him say invitingly aside to the antique Professor the other day—his cap askew, attractively light on his feet for a man of his age and girth. His ship was as easy with him as his dog. It would bite strangers, but crouch to him. She was going up to see around the sea from that bridge, though, and she was going that very morning. The Captain paused socially by a group of passengers on the deck; and you'd be tactful with a man who held his head aloof that way, even if his sailor's cap had a flippant rake. He was talking and making fun with them, while screwing with finger and thumb the point of his neat little creamy beard. You could see that though he was affable with his passengers he was thinking of something else. His white uniform made his big jowls so florid, such rosy flanks to his face, that they undid the severity of his nose. Could Drake ever die?

Whatever was that? It was another ship, if it were real. Round the point of the island a barque had appeared. How did it get there? You'd have said it had been created in an instant out of sea and mist. It was both. That sail-ship was a leisurely and shining roller ridden by a cloud. It surged upwards and on. She expected it to rise clear of the water. Its head lifted lightly as though the impulse had come to fly. It was off. Then it bowed and buried itself in the sea, and the sea sent up a spurt of white vapour to join the lofty cloud above. The barque heeled, and a flash of vermilion came from its body. Was it fire and water and mist? Mrs. Travers forgot the captain and the group of passengers. She felt she ought to cheer. She stood at the rail, forgetful of herself, her finger-tips just resting on her own ship, and rising on her toes in unconscious response. She was astonished by a masterpiece.

The Captain turned and saw her. There was Mrs. Travers. She hardly ever spoke at table, but he knew that when she peeped over at him in gay disbelief she could quicken his enjoyment in his own nonsense. His romantic affection had been stirred by the buoyancy and brightness of that barque; it recalled his youth. Mrs. Travers, trim and rare, as he saw her intent on the lustrous shape in the distance, was in accord with that memory. He left the others.

"Isn't she a beauty, Mrs. Travers?"

She had nothing to say. Her agreement was only a laugh of enjoyment.

The barque had passed. Now the sea was as empty as though nothing could happen there; only the island winked. Mantell came up; and as the Captain appraised that young man's admirable shape, and glanced from it to Mrs. Travers, the romantic stirring of his past suffered from the regretful admonition of age. Who, he speculated to himself, is Travers, to leave this girl about? Not that the careless fellow need worry, perhaps.

"Did you see the barque pass us, Mr. Mantell?" said the Captain.

"I didn't. I was below." Mantell was indifferent. "You are coming ashore, Mrs. Travers?"

"No."

"Why, not to see one of the island of the pirates? Not to see where the treasure is hidden?"

"No."

Mantell hesitated; he seemed disappointed. The Captain was comically solemn. "Your pirate stuff doesn't interest Mrs. Travers, you can see. Why should she bother about old treasure stowed away nobody knows where?" He thought his question was a nice success. He was pleased. Mrs. Travers had searched his eyes, and flushed.

With his lady passenger, the Captain surveyed the departure of the shore party. Mantell waved to Mrs. Travers from the launch; the two girls with him vivaciously acknowledged only the ship's master above them. He called down some dry absurdities to them. The launch swerved away for the island.

"Well, that's that. It's a full party; they're glad to get aboard us, but always glad of any excuse to get away again. It's a quiet ship to ourselves. Mr. Adamson will be in my room waiting for me—you haven't met him? Come along. The engineer. Ballast tanks and engines and complaints and all sorts of Scotch stuff to discuss that wouldn't interest you. But you must meet Adamson. Glasgow made him. Come away up with me. Come and have a look round from the top side."

Later, when reading in her cabin, waiting for the dinner bugle—the frivolity of the cocktail groups in the smokeroom was not highly amusing—Mrs. Travers, inattentive to the page, became aware of the renewed pulsations of the heart of the ship. They were murmuring and subdued. The ship was alive again. You had to close your eyes to be quite sure of the driving life that was hidden.

She was on her way to Santa Maria. The ship had a heart, like everybody else, but Mr. Adamson only said "aye," very cautiously, when she told him so that morning. He wasn't in the least gratified. He had a gaunt face like a mastiff who sadly disbelieves your kindly interest. "Aye. Ther's some wad ca' it a hairt, and ther's some wad ca' it a rummel in their ain heid. It's engines."

The Captain had chuckled. "Now I'll tell you, Mrs. Travers. The Chief is more sentimental than you are. I've seen the tears roll down his rugged cheeks—late at night, mind you—when he heard 'Annie Laurie' on my gramophone. It's too early in the day to try it on

him—the Scotch never cry in the morning—but one
night I'll turn on the record for you, and you'll see
it's as good as Harry Lauder."

The Chief did not deny it. It was no matter what
was said by one who was not an engineer, when the
subject was engines. The Captain filled up Mrs. Adamson's glass again. "Much more sentimental than a
pretty girl with a soft heart, only he likes you to think
he is ruled by numbers. You know what I mean, the
inevitability of necessity. Hearts are bunk."

"Nay, nay. That'll nay dae. Hairts are like turbines.
It's necessity. They canna' help themselves, puir
bodies."

The bugle! That was only the noise of dinner;
rightly they should bang a soup tureen. For you could
not get used to a bugle; it turned the diaphragm pale.
That shrill call was always to the adventure of a new
life. Now all the closed doors of the corridors were
opening, and the just and the unjust were resurrecting
to the judgment, conscious of new dresses and critical
eyes in the light of the grand saloon.

The Captain was solid in his chair. Dinner had a
greater interest when you could have it beside so assured a weight of experience and shrewdness—yes, she
guessed, and an explosive force in the middle of it—

but who could disguise it in fun. Mantell was striding round the tables, late as usual, and now they'd hear about the pirates. Yet perhaps they would not; he could be as discreet as a dummy, when he chose.

What a dress! That black-haired girl, and a sheath of silver scales! Well, you'd have to admit her slim figure was delightful. She could safely wait till nearly everybody had arrived, and then serpentine glittering to her table. Yet whatever did she talk about, to those she knew? Perhaps Mantell could say, if he were asked. It didn't matter. She could walk in a way that made others appear to mince and hobble along. In that metallic reptilian skin she would be worth watching when dancing tonight.

Mantell was telling his neighbour what a good novel he was reading.

Oh yes, bantered the Captain. Is that what you were doing when the barque passed us this morning? Reading a novel? I'd have betted you were. All this talk of literature—that and scandal! On a ship like this, doing the summer islands, a sailor never hears anything else at his dinner. And I've noticed literature is always novels. They're all about life, aren't they? I know it —the sort of life sailors who don't care are supposed to have when not at home, like me. But when the

thing itself is going by, the real thing worth understanding, what are you doing? Reading about it—too
busy to move.

Mantell declared he was not. He was moving vigorously. As it happened, he was hunting for a collar
stud—it had rolled under the bunk, right to the back.
Besides, he wasn't a sailor.

My dear sir, is it necessary to be a sailor before you
can recognize a good thing when it is there? I thought
Oxford could do more for you than that. You people
who get it out of books don't know the truth when
it's under your noses, unless it is in print. And what
is it when it's that? Only a place to put a bookmark,
while you look for a lost stud.

Now the two of them were busy. This would last a
long time. The Professor would join in, after the
sounds at the table had soaked through his abstraction.
His expansion of the talk would carry to the coffee,
and, if you were pleased to follow the Professor to the
smokeroom afterwards, continue to any distance.
What do you think about it, Mrs. Travers? Well, she
didn't think about it.

The Professor heard that. What's that? Not think?
Quite right, don't you do it. It's dangerous. Don't you

think. We should get a chance to see where our trouble began if we didn't do so much thinking.

Speak for yourself, said the Captain. I speak for everybody, the Professor told him. I've lived long enough to see that thinking is the curse of the world. People never do it until they intend to behave badly, or want to make the result of imbecility look quite good. Then they go to it, and you're almost persuaded that an awful mess came simply of following the same law as apple-trees, and was twice as natural. Thinking has made the world what it is. And how do you like it?

The Captain grumbled; like hell. The Professor said it was the same thing. And, he added, if you reason it out, you can easily prove that nothing else was possible, so we were meant to get hell. What's more, it can be shown logically that God thinks the same about it as ourselves; which may be so, for all you or I know. Unless, of course, he gave us reason to play with, so that we may cut our throats with it, if we want to.

Professor, you ought not to say that. Mrs. Binney spoke earnestly. She was the wife of the principal owner of the line. You had to be careful with her; but she was an old dear, and was aware that a touch or two of peril didn't do the children any harm.

All right, Mrs. Binney, said the Professor. You

won't report me to the dean of my university, will you? He must keep right with money, and so must I. But between ourselves, strictly as one friend to another, tell me whether you don't worry because the society by which we get our money looks no better than a stack of awkward junk piled sky-high by a solemn idiot? It gives me the trembles to look at it. And while waiting for the tottering mass to brain me, there am I, when at home, justifying the noble but desperate edifice to the innocent. But not here. We're not innocent. We're on a holiday.

"And are you trying to persuade us to be happy on a holiday?" asked the Captain. "But listen to me, Professor. If I don't do a bit of thinking on the bridge after supper, you may have to swim ashore in your nightshirt."

Here was the cherub himself from aloft, in a sailor's suit, standing at the Captain's elbow. That silenced the table. The Captain read the radiogram, and put it in his pocket. He wouldn't satisfy your legitimate interest, not if there were another ship on fire. He would coolly pick up the loose end of the talk where he had left it.

Take my advice, Mrs. Travers, he whispered now, never you be a ship's master. You might as well be a telephone operator. A sailor's was always a dog's life, but now he's a dog on a chain. The other end of the chain is held by a clerk in an office thousands of miles away. He can choke you off your food. I tell you the invention of wireless has worried more men to death than it ever saved. Try this savoury. It's jolly good. What is it called?

This is queer, she thought. New York has just spoken to this man beside her, and has said something he didn't like; yet in the Caribbean Sea they had seemed enclosed within the yellow glow of the lamps on their intimate table.

She looked up. She caught sight of the open port in the white wall of the ship beside them; the tropic night, the outer world, was only a delicious purple round, no bigger than a dinner plate, but infinitely deep and obscure.

Did fate have an eye like that, when it looked at you—as soft and mild as that of an old cow chewing the cud, and just as meaningless, until your hour struck? You would hardly notice that it was constant above your table, that eye, overlooking the chattering, till then. Then you had to leave the others; you had to go. The Captain was going now.

On deck you could believe they were all supported

in the dark by nothing but the pale spook of their ship. Suppose that were to fade away absolutely? It had lost its body. What was left was a glimmer on odd lengths of its white shape. That glimmer held together enough of the deck for them to dance on. They could just see where they would vanish, if they did not turn towards their jazz music again. All the Spanish Main was no more than a low humming, and you had to listen for that.

She looked overside. There was no more sea. There were swaths of pale fire. Their ship was in a cauldron of greenish flames which gave no light.

It was hardly more comforting to turn inwards towards the mulatto saxophonists, but nothing else was left for you to do. When your faith weakens you fly to jazz, and mock midnight. The musicians, as they played, waved about their braying instruments in derisive abandon, and with smiles of cunning benevolence. One was tapping with his foot, beguiling them to it. That jazz music was the funny bleating of poor little bolsheviks too timid to do anything but dance, so it was the right music for them. She leaned against the bulwarks, in the shadow, and watched the dancing of the girl in the scaly sheath.

Heavens! if that girl would only let herself go, go

like mad, instead of slithering round to the music of people who could not make up their minds to anything important! She was entwined with Mantell, but she never flashed boldly unless her imitation scales happened to pass near a lamp.

That number was finished. Mantell could have danced with more decision and purpose, if the measure had been positive. And now he was looking for her. Mrs. Travers remained within the shadow—edged more securely into it; moved off quickly under its cover along the deck, and went below to her cabin.

Chapter Twenty-five

THE LONGER THEY WERE AT SEA, THE DEEPER INTO THE distance Santa Maria receded. Mantell never mentioned the place now. It had not been confirmed for some time. The idea of it now was more indistinct than when she began the voyage. It was less real than one of those tiny islands on the horizon which the Captain said nobody ever visited because nothing was there.

Nothing? How forlorn they looked! A ship should go to that one they were pointing to now. But nothing was there. Nobody ever went to it. Their ship would pass by it. All you could make out was a trifling blot on the straight line dividing the water from the sky. It would be dreadful if one unlucky man were there, and saw them pass, even as the other ships passed him, each of them sure that nothing was there.

Santa Maria was less than that. What was it? She could arrive, she had been told, before he could leave the country. That was as certain as official print when she first read the Minister's radiogram to Mantell.

What was it now? For the voyage had enlarged the earth, made it multiple, difficult, and uncertain. And sometimes nothing was there. Therefore that region from which, she was told, he could not easily get away? Why, was it as huge as all that? Because the insignificant islands, many of which were never visited, dotted the sea each day, and all day, and the sea appeared capable of infinite expansion; no matter how much of it was left behind, it remained the same ahead and around. Paranagua was a name that sounded like a deep noise far away at night.

So she asked the Captain about Santa Maria. What, our last port, my dear? That is only an anchorage, but it isn't like any you've seen. It's the mainland. It's the beginning of a new world, and only an end to our cruise, where we turn back. And glad to do it. He didn't care much for Santa Maria.

Once he got fever at that place. He was a youngster then, in sails. They were anchored there too long. He had fever and nearly died. Some of the other fellows weren't so lucky, and they're at Santa Maria now. He seldom took his ship there, and wouldn't worry if he never did again, after this trip.

Why? Well, he could hardly explain it. Perhaps because he nearly went out there, as a young man, with

Yellow Jack. Nasty fellow, that, and generally hanging around in that land. Perhaps he didn't like it because he never cared much for grand opera.

That continent was mighty serious and important; that's what he meant by grand opera. Of course, the stuff is all right if you know what it's about, but it confused him. He was only a sailor. He couldn't keep up with it. It didn't seem natural. You see, you don't know what is at the back of Santa Maria, and if you ask they make a splendid song about it, which he thought was foolishness. Anyhow, you don't see through it.

Now, my girl, if you touch at one of these islands, like Jamaica, where it is bright and breezy and every nigger is laughing, you know where you are and there's nothing to bother you. You'll see. It's fun. There's nothing to get you all balled up, as the saying goes. You know it is good to be there. But Santa Maria is solemn because only God knows all about it, and you can't tell what will happen. If you go into the beyond, that means months, and you don't come out the same way, if ever you come out. It's a great country, though; yes, it's a wonderful land, that. But you'd better return in my ship, my dear, or you'll get lost. Why, Santa Maria is only the first verse of the first chapter of Genesis, as you might say. It's too much for me, at my age.

"But what are you going to do at Santa Maria, Mrs. Travers, if I may ask? It's no place for a lady."

"I'm going to meet my husband."

"Are you! That's another story. Why didn't you say so at first? He'll look after you. I should say Santa is quite all right for you, if you don't stay there too long . . . Let's see. Isn't Mr. Mantell going there, too?"

"Yes. He's a friend of Mr. Travers's."

The steamer did not hurry. She might have been as adverse from Paranagua as her master. She was leisurely at her ports of call, lengthening the voyage. The days and islands began to run together, so you couldn't be sure whether it was Wednesday or Guadeloupe; but as there were more islands than days it was fairly certain to be neither.

Some of the islands were immense green cones, each straight up to its own cloud; and some were desert shores, long and low, burnt to craggy yellow, and no shade from a bare sun. And one was a big topaz— which one was that? It was a beauty. The blaze of the sea about it was like the beginning of the earth. Their steamer politely lay off, as the Captain said; and quite properly, too. No iron ship could swim in a furnace where sheets of emeralds, amethysts, and lapis were fusing. She felt like Eve in the distance, watching and waiting while one little bit of earth's mosaic was being completed; she was as young as that. All things were still to come. There was to be an immense fulfilment. Only the floor was being laid.

Ah, time! For it was easy to remember moments—such a moment as that. Was that because moments are of chief importance? Moments are life? Let us say days of the week, and names, do not count. We begin to count the years only when we are perplexed, when we have become fearful because of so much that is past. A muddle always has the grey look of age, of time lost.

Well, tempus does fugit, much too fast, especially after you have stopped to look back. You have spent a fair amount of it. You can see that. The more you've had of it, the quicker you lose it. Then you become greedy. You want to save it, you want it to slow down, because you fear the moments in it are fewer than they used to be. She felt that sudden dismay yesterday, through watching the sunset—always a romantic and foolish intermission. She had an idea there would be an event, because the evening vault was cleared. A dem-

onstration was coming. The sun was hanging detached
from the cold west, a globe without a ray, for his fire
was only enough for himself; his fire was pulsing
feebly within its own round, uncertain of holding long
enough. Then the sun fell. His fire would not hold
out. He fell through the last of his journey into the
black sea as though tired of making day. Done with it!
He sank into the blackness, and was extinguished instantly. Gone before her surprise! He had no reflections; he had forgotten everything. It was night at
once.

Time flew! She had seen some of it run out, in the
very act. Dear God, need it go as fast as that?

She glanced aft along the deck then, for the sight
of another human being, for assurance, for comfort.
The deck stretched away like a chill and empty desert,
with grey menace around. Nobody else was there
—yes, a sailor was at the extremity of the ship, so far
away that he was only an indistinct figure, the last
man, hauling down the ensign. Hauling it down!

Don't haul it down, sailor. Sunset is when it should
be flown. The ensign isn't needed in the morning.
After dark, nail it to the mast.

Chapter Twenty-six

SHE PAUSED, WHEN ON THE STAIRS GOING BELOW. Either while her mind was absent her feet were idling down without caring where they went, or else the stairway had turned giddy. Be careful, miss, said a passing steward, she's rolling a little.

On her first long voyage, Mrs. Travers had made a discovery. When she closed her cabin door till morning, that act had a hint of finality, of parting from the world, of the last act; good-bye to everybody! The ship as a minor planet held its course among the stars, carrying the quick and the dead; and she had gone apart from its life. Now she had only herself to face.

It was not strange that some people shrank from the severance. Mrs. Binney confided to her that she would never stay in her cabin alone for an hour, if she could help it; and that was odd in so tranquil a woman. What was she afraid of? You do indeed need resolution to gaze frankly at the mirror in solitude—and now she did so she didn't feel she had need to fear yet—

and at the same time hear nothing of the outer life, nothing but its undertones telling you it is still resolved and busy; but no more than that. You don't know what it is doing. Do you care? You cannot be sure that you do not. What is it doing? Is all well?

She guessed now why it was that John flinched so nervously from sociability. He probably knew that affable and cosy chatter blurred one's outlines. You are melted into a common lump of warm and sticky cordiality. You cannot be yourself. If he were in that ship it would take a deal of her blarney to get him to leave their cabin. She didn't think she would be inclined to use much of it, either. No, she would let him have his way, to a reasonable extent. She stood by her bunk, considering the implications of that.

It was an age since last she saw him. Had he changed? He had not. John was the same as ever, only considerably worse. Something told her that John, whatever happened, would be at the very end but the logical testimony to his beginning. It was like him to hold straight on—as do, of course, the lunatics; nothing changes them, either.

The ship heaved, and the undertone of its progress towards Santa became more pronounced than a murmur. It rose to a rumbling growl. She took two steps to recover her balance, and steadied. The steamer had behaved like a porpoise. She had never heard of bad weather in those tropical seas.

She knew well enough that when a man said with the complacency of plenary inspiration that he understood a woman that he was a fool, so she thought it fair to assume that a woman might possibly misunderstand a man. John was a child, with his mild questioning eyes, and that part of him was easy. She could play with it. But there was no doubt that he was deeper than any sin could possibly be. He had the eyes of an innocent, but was as old as Egypt. What could a woman do with a creature who was as immemorial and still as that?

The ship certainly was growing very restless. It was distracting, to totter on a rocking floor with one's usual right thoughts. She didn't want anything else to think about. That occasional growl of the ship, when it trembled, shook thoughts to their centre.

She would turn in and read. Perhaps she could read. Very decidedly the lamp could not be turned out when the ship was uttering the annoyance of a big animal seriously disturbed. She must do something. She listened for voices in the corridor.

It was silent. Nobody was about. All was well. She

wasn't used to the sea, that was all. She sighed, and considered her circumstances. There waiting was that book which John always kept beside his bed. But she had not brought it to read; she had brought it only as a reminder, just to cheer her up. Was it a good omen? Though he rarely made a mistake when he recommended a book, he had never invited her to read that one. The omission was queer, now it was noticed, for as a rule the same author pleased both of them. No, he had never mentioned this book. She stared pensively into vacancy, and listened, as she opened it, sighed again, and tried to bend her attention to its secret.

> "If this I did not every moment see,
> And if my thoughts did stray
> At any time, or idly play,
> And fix on other objects, yet
> This Apprehension set
> In me
> Was all my whole felicity."

She read that twice. What did it mean? She sought elsewhere in the little volume for this magical apprehension. She would use it at once. Perhaps invariably it lost its potency in a ship; you had other apprehensions then. It appeared to be a devotional book; but

John's religion, so far as she knew it, could not be left about by a bishop for the children to play with. She turned the pages, but it seemed the apprehension was nimbler than her fingers. It was over leaf before she could catch it.

Reading was of no use. She might have expected that, when a ship had noises even harder to understand than shadowy poetry. Something alive, she began to imagine, was stealthy beneath the berth. She peered over to see, and just saved herself from toppling when the ship rolled over till the fear came that this time it could not recover. A dressing-case shot from under the berth and brought up against the side. She waited. Was everything breaking loose? The cabin steadily reversed.

Mrs. Travers was reluctant to ring for her stewardess, but she wished to know. She wished to hear a reasonable voice. It was midnight. Should she ring, or was that cowardly? She shuddered, as did the very cabin, at a shock like the burst of a gun, and then another roll began. . . was prolonged! She rang her bell boldly without caring whether it was cowardly or not.

How long the stewardess was in answering! Was there anyone left to answer? Or was she the only one forgotten? She braced herself to endure this. She was getting used to endurance—she had been staid and cheerful and hardly knew that it was virtuous. Morning usually comes, if you wait long enough. By strictly noting every movement she fancied the ship was easier. Perhaps she had been prematurely foolish; courage, though, ought not to be unfairly tested, and for too long. An immediate thudding, and a sound of heavy clambering against her port light, sent her from her berth precipitously. She put on her dressing-gown in readiness. She would have to act. She could not lie there in patience till morning, and not know. Let patience go! How long had she been patient? This was more than enough, after so long.

She opened her cabin door, and peered out. The corridor was lighted, but strangely empty. The far end of it rose to a steep incline as she watched. The door there leading to the deck was open, and as she wondered what was in the dark beyond it a mass of water plunged through and the torrent charged down and swept past her feet. She was so surprised that she did not cry out. She met it dismayed, but resigned.

A passenger flung from his room and raced to a struggle with the door. Not till the corridor inclined the other way did the door surrender unexpectedly; it slammed, dragging him headlong after it, strong as he was. He swore, and turned about with an angry face. The interlude was so unaffected and ordinary that she laughed; and she heard for herself that her amusement was immoderate.

"Damned fools," explained Mantell, "to leave it open. Surely you weren't going to shut it?"

She shook her head. She knew it would be unwise for her to speak. Nor did he speak again, but stood in doubt. Her laughter had not been her own. He wondered whether this quest was trying her too severely. He could see it was. Her nerves were going.

Damn that man! If Travers could see his wife now it would bring him to his senses. She was enough to bring any man to his senses . . . if it wasn't for Travers! He ought to tell her to go to bed again. There was nothing to worry about. All was well. But he was uncertain of the right words.

Mrs. Travers was quicker than he. With an ironic but merry grimace she was stepping back into her cabin, and then the ship lurched. Mantell caught and held her as she overbalanced. She made no effort to recover herself.

Chapter Twenty-seven

IN THEIR FLIGHT FROM THE TOWN OF ZARAZA, THE three refugees could see that the way out of it, as they must take it, was hardly more attractive than the streets of the town. While they stood considering the dizzy ascent of escape before beginning upon it, the engineer encouraged the bo'sun, and was blithe. He admitted the bo'sun was right, that the track would be easier for birds. But there it was, all they would get. For himself, he would rather give that climb a chance than be a feed for dogs. Hadn't they seen the dogs feeding in the streets?

The bo'sun did remember them, but was still unconvinced between ghoulish dogs and a wall that seemed unscalable. That path, he said, if it was a path, did not remind him of any way down to the sea that he knew of. Sure it was right?

His friend chuckled. No, you wouldn't expect to find a ship on top of it; though the other end of it, if they ever reached it—and they might, if they didn't stand there talking till some loving patriots of Paranagu came along—was more like ships. The railroad was out of use, except for excursions with a field-gun, and there had been no excursions since the breech-block blew out. And there they were.

The track shimmering over them in the heat could be distinguished, with care, in high and unrelated parts of the precipice. They could pick out short lengths of it inclined amid the perpendicular scrub and yellow crags and bosses, but with no sign of continuity. The sun was blazing on it to the distant cleft, an insignificant blue notch of sky, where the track went over the brow. The engineer indicated it as though it was a funny instance. The face of the steep glowed and quivered. The engineer said it smelt as hot as a new brass casting, but it had a merit for him. It hadn't so much reform about it as Zaraza, where you couldn't tell a pay-office from an ambush. Always live on, if you can.

Travers, the higher they mounted, felt his weight the less. For the first few hundred feet the heat rang in his ears. He thought his heart would burst. The cliff itself was radiant. He doubted that he could get his body to the top. When he glanced up, breathless and too soon, to measure how much was left of this toil, that upper nick of blue was no nearer; it had gone. Above him was only an overhang of brazen rock, with a vine pendant from it, a rope dangling beyond reach in midair. The threat of that mass bulging beyond the point of rest, which startled him when he paused to wipe the sweat from his eyes, gave him the sense that the mountain-side itself was reeling over the void like his own head.

He took the next step; he went on, and presently grew lighter, and forgot it. His anxiety to get this over left him. His deliberate hands and feet began to feel in the steep earth an assurance of inherent stability, however repellent and impossible the distance appeared to be. With his nose near the ground, scanning every foot of it as he mounted, he became aware of its fine texture, of small and secret things in it which amused him with a hint that his illusion of present time came only of his fear of breaking his neck while taking careful steps in a crawl over the face of eternity. Once he noticed the whorl of a sea-shell, a fossil in the limestone, for this was an old sea-floor, this mountain; and beside that shell was the rosette of an alpine plant in blue flower on the dry limestone, the very seal of credence. He was with them both; the span of infinity was between his finger and thumb. They told him that

no more than the next step is ever needed in any enterprise. The other steps come in their turn; a chosen
path secludes them till necessity shows where they are,
and the sum of it is as an alpine plant celebrating the
goodness of the sea-floor, all to be seen in a glance.

Even that notch of sky in the summit, so remote and
evasive that it had been in another place whenever he
had looked up in doubt, even that could be trusted.
The three men at length rested in it, finding shade, for
the tiny notch was a deep gorge, and its walls towered.
They surveyed Zaraza in the plain below, and in its
turn that town had taken on its relative significance.
Its slag heaps, black and grotesque mining structures,
and sporadic sheds and buildings had run together, and
were no more than one of man's chance blots in a
luminous universe, except that the three watchers
knew why smoke was rolling away from it.

"See that? That's what reformers think of my en-
gine-house," commented the American. "There it
goes. Better days are marching on." He kissed his hand
to the smoke.

They descended a valley, and in the bottom, by a
stream, came to a few huts. An Indian potter was at his
wheel. The old man turned his face to the intrusion,
and then continued his work as if some leaves had

rustled down into his clearing. The silent women and children about him behaved as though unaware that strangers had come. The engineer went up to the native, brusquely, if friendly, for he wanted news of this part of the land. The Indian paused, but was taciturn. He appeared not to know that war was about him, nor to care if it were.

Travers stood apart relishing the scene. It was framed with high dark trees, and the sun brimmed the enclosure, as a well, with bright peace. It belonged to the earth and smelt of it. That was the fresh clay. The feet of the slow brown figures were grey with it; they had grown out of it. An odorous bark was smouldering. The new buff pots were a heap of melons, gourds, and pumpkins, just the shapes you would expect, for they must take the prompting of the mould. Some of them were ornamented with black and red zigzags. But for their freshness they could have come from a stone-age mound; they were the direct outcome of the wares of the men who lived before the kings and priests. What age was this place? It went at an invisible pace. It was outside the almanac.

He, too, stood outside. Circumstances always gave him that apprehension, that he was present, yet apart, looking on; that all about him was going out with the tide, was leaving him. There was no peace that abided, and no friends. Yet this enclosure would last his day. He enjoyed it because of that. It was nearer to being at rest. He held away one shapely pot on his palm, the better to see it.

The engineer was derisive. "That truck breaks," he said. "They're not much used now, not now there's petrol-cans. This old boy is a poor dummy, making these things. I suppose he's got nothing else to do."

Travers continued to eye the shape. "You can't break that," he told the engineer, to that man's astonishment. "You can't break that. It's an idea. He has shaped it, and we've seen it. How can you break that? It exists. You can only break the pot."

"That's what I mean," grinned the engineer. "You drop it, and what is it? Now, it don't matter if you drop a petrol-can."

Travers was laughing to himself over that as they splashed through the stream, on their way. They entered the woods. His amusement puzzled the engineer, who glanced over his shoulder at Travers, to make sure he really was tickled by the thought that a dropped can is obliging. It was something, anyway, to have made that queer guy laugh. Nobody could have guessed he could laugh. It wasn't easy to amuse a man who went outside to sit by the cold rocks all night after he had been led to a most hospitable house and an alluring bed. The engineer had wondered sometimes whether Travers had any feeling, or was merely nuts. That man could keep going on when he and the sailor were whacked to the wide. How did he do it? And it was all right to pay no attention to other men's bullets when you were shooting off your own, but how was a fellow made who looked on, doing nothing, because the shower couldn't pelt for ever? There was nothing the matter with the sailor. The sailor had sense. When the trouble was too big to handle he stood off; but he could make some for himself, like any other man, if there was a chance to get away with it.

The engineer supposed they could make the coast, the line they were on, in a few days, unless one of them cracked. They were not likely to see anything but trees, not on that trail. Nobody used it. Did he know it? Sure he knew it—he had been along it once before, and no time to waste, after killing a man. He got to the coast then in thirty hours, for an alibi, but it was a record, and it would never be beaten.

When they began another climb, crawling on all fours up a tunnel through the forest, so dank and lumbered with fallen stuff that it was no better than struggling through the foundation rubbish of a murky vastness beyond the comprehension of ants lost in its nameless litter, the engineer, in a pause for breath, picking thorns out of his body, said this was only a taste. How did they like it? There were jollier bits further on. He couldn't make out how he got through so easily, that other time. He must have had something else to think about. It only showed you—when you have something big on your mind you don't worry about the prickles. That country was more like God's awful scrap-heap than a finished product.

The bo'sun patiently examined a weal on his arm, the bite of an insect. He agreed with the engineer. "You must be more than right. Didn't you say there were only trees here? What do you call this?" He peered dubiously into the greenish dusk but was resigned. The rummy thing was that the guv'nor didn't seem to care. Bert took careful stock of Mr. Travers, on the quiet. He looked all right, taking it easy, just like a stroll in the park, this was, and he knew all about closing time, and the short cut to the gates.

The bo'sun, when they were working through it again, at times turned his head to the backward track, expecting to surprise the hush, which was too strange to be good; he felt he might catch it in artful movements behind them, for the queer shapes were ugly, if fixed. He never saw anything shift an inch, nor heard a rustle, which was entirely wrong. Ugly things are worse when they watch without moving. Now, in a gale, with hatches adrift, you know where you are and what to expect next, besides which there's a noise to shout against.

Even when they emerged into a higher and more open land in sunlight, and from a superior embrasure in the tangle could survey immense gulfs of lower forest to other ramparts, and to ranges far enough away in the heat of the sky to be beyond human consideration, Bert was less at ease than when under fire in Zaraza. The unknown was fearful, reflecting the dark of his mind. That engineer, though, was a man, he recognized. That fellow wore the belt, and was welcome to it; the engineer gave the landscape only short and sneering notice, about as much as was needed to see his way through the foul stuff and to free its knots. It was just a nuisance to work through. Yet he sweated, and the guv'nor didn't.

Yet Travers, who appeared indifferent, was only still. He was aware of no scrap-heap, and of nothing fearful, but kept his own counsel. He saw the world with his own eyes, but knew that could be darkness to others. He was untroubled, for he had no doubts, and was in no hurry, either to escape, or to come to a reckoning. He was only surprised; he thought he saw the earth for the first time. About him was the shining original. He knew why God saw that it was good; he could see that himself. Man could, if he chose, be the only despoiler of this, its only impediment, or else could throne himself upon it, when he knew its light, and was able to bear it. So Travers was buoyant, released from all within. Surprised by a vision of the extravagant undertaking of life in a manifold world, he knew he would be upborne, though he were on a height with no support but his trust, for he felt no misgiving. Morass, forest, mountain shelf, and the ocean of the woods below running in billows to indefinition and over the round of the globe, the same yesterday, today, and forever, were but the semblance of his own conviction, the show of infinity, the sign of the continuity of the glory of the earth. He was not separate. He had no submission to make to that show of power, for he was part of it. He felt he could outlast the present shadows of it, see the pale dilation of the Sierras waver and die on the sky, that he could outlive the sun; yet the power which gave him peace would be there.

They came in sight of the Caribbean. The three travellers, rounding a bastion in their path, were brought to a halt, and gazed down to a nether sky beyond the distant serpentining filament which marked the end of the land.

Was it the sea? If not, what was it? For the verge of the land was distinct, if delicate, but space beyond it, like the conviction which supported Travers on a height, was bottomless.

The bo'sun grunted, and began to fill his pipe. He was satisfied. Now he saw something that he knew. The engineer grinned; he remarked, after gratifying himself with his contemplation of the vast proof of his success, that they had made good time.

Travers nodded his ready and cheerful assent to his companions. He was happy to have found the sea; they had made it in good time. Yet what contented him was the still apparition of perpetuity, which was blue, like space. Space and time had merged. He could see the sober reality. Still, he could agree with the engineer that his watch was correct. You choose for your existence your own dimension, and keep it, while allowing other people to keep theirs, so that their reckoning may not be confused by yours.

He was early abroad next morning. Travers was always the first to stir. The bo'sun complained that Mr. Travers never slept, and went missing. Before sunrise he left the house to which the engineer had taken them. Santa Maria was but a day's march away, and the rebellion was over.

He threaded his way through a plantation which was asleep, and was nearly discernible. He wished to be present in the only hour in the tropical day which is fresh and glad. The trees in lane between the villas were beginning to come out of night in vague forms. Solid shadows that were leaves hung heavy with dew. It was hard to tell whether he was in the twilight of the forgotten, which no call could ever bring back to the sun, or whether this was all to be born, and was waiting to quicken at a word.

An arc of sky became dusky saffron, and the superior crowns of some royal palms were inky flourishes upon it. The saffron burned quickly to clear gold, and at once shrubs and lower leaves were personal about him, as though the word had come. A pungent smell rose warmly from the earth. A solitary bird meditated aloud.

Travers stood in a grove, leaning against a palm trunk in a pool of night not yet removed, and looked across a glittering lawn to a row of cannas which bor-

dered it in coloured flames. A woman stepped from
that house. Her poise and gait shook his memory; but
in that filmy white dress and with that rich complexion he supposed she was native, like the cannas and
the smell of earth. A broad hat shaded her face. She
was young.

He did not move. A thought from the past perplexed him, without shape. The woman stood in the
morning garden, vivid and gracious, a legendary form,
and her gown was diaphanous with the east beyond it.
She glanced at the sky, perhaps saw the tropic day
was too young to be unkind, and whipped off her hat.
Well he knew that gesture. She ran a hand over her
hair, and turned to look at the house. Her upturned
profile was traced by the new light.

He was startled. His hand began to wander to his
face, but he checked it. He did not move. Fanny Travers turned, in the brightness of a morning from which
he was withdrawn, and looked at the house, expectant.
A door in the upper veranda opened, and a young man
came to the rail, rested his hands upon it, and spoke
banteringly down to Fanny. Travers did not hear her
answer, but it was merry.

The big fellow flung himself over the rail, and
dropped, with the liberty of an athlete. Travers ob-

served it as though it were a scene predestined on a stage illuminated and withdrawn. The two met, and greeted, joining their hands, laughing and swinging them like happy children in playful intimacy, and then strolled away into the shrubbery beyond. The stage was empty again.

He could see they would withhold nothing from each other. Who was that man? He remembered him somehow—a ship—Liverpool—no; he had forgotten. His name did not matter. Those two looked well together, in this play apart.

The unseen bird continued to meditate aloud, and he could hear Fanny's voice. They were in accord. He continued to watch the empty stage. Would he see her there again? Should he seek her? An impulse came over him, but at once failed.

He did not move. He could not walk into that sunlight. It was alien, in a world removed. He could never enter it again. It belonged to those who were in it, living another life than he knew. He had gone from it. He had departed. There was no return for him to the day in which they moved.

Chapter Twenty-eight

"AND WHAT'S MORE," THE BO'SUN WAS ARGUING, "what good will you do? I can't see it."

Bert had made up his mind. He was becoming a little desperate. He would have to stop the guv'nor at this game. It would be really asking for it; more dangerous than Zaraza. Gun-fire is one thing—that's a matter of luck; but all his experience warned him that it is fatal to stroll into the running machinery, which attends to fools immediately. And when you came down to it, what was the guv'nor after? He wasn't a fool, so what did he want to do?

Bert was not so clear about that; yet he was sure, from as much as he could make of it, that it would be about as useful as when a sacked stoker stands in the head-office and stiffs and blinds the unseen chairman and directors of a royal mail line. What happens then? A bald-headed bookkeeper turns rusty, and sends for the police.

Bert was anxious. They were getting near to Colonna, that island where people were busy on what the guv'nor said was wrong.

Well, what of it? Suppose it was! Lots of things are wrong. You can't stop them. If old Snarge, that shipowner and lord almighty, had got his talons on that island for a reason he knew all about, and you didn't, then it didn't matter a damn what you thought about it.

And there was Mr. Travers now, leaning on the ship's rail, admiring the coast in the distance, as free and easy as a tourist getting used to his first trip. He ought to know better, after what he had been through. It was all very well, but you'll never stop the powers that boss the show from doing what they want to do. They have always done it. You have to take it, and if you don't grouse about it they let you live, sometimes. You can't stop the ship by kicking at a bulkhead.

The guv'nor didn't see that. He wouldn't listen to sense. He was worse than a shipowner. He was like a child. All he did was to smile as if he knew he was down in his rich grandfather's will.

And if he did say anything about it, what was it? The same as the words on a valentine, as near as the bo'sun could fathom it. They were good words, but what did that matter? What Mr. Travers talked about was not down in the chart. It was off the map. It had no bearings, and you couldn't pick it up. The stuff was all right to listen to, if you understood it, but you couldn't make it fast to anything handy to hold your weight. It wouldn't bear weight.

Another few days and they'd be at that island, and weather permitting there they'd land. That island was only about five by six, so the pair of them would stand out as plain as two blue-bottles buzzing on a window. They'd be swotted. Of course they would. It was monkeying with the Government.

The two men were leaning on the rail of an Italian coasting steamer, going south, then midway between Messina and Catania. Travers was watching the coast, picking up landmarks. They were abreast of the site of Naxos. That was where the Greeks founded their first city in Sicily. There were signs above it of Tauromenium, that eyrie in the crags.

"Bert," said Travers, "what's that word you sailors use, kenspeckled? I like that word. It's a jolly one."

The bo'sun mumbled that so far as he was concerned that coast yonder wasn't kenspeckled, and he didn't care. He didn't know it. Give him the Bristol Channel. Hartland Point two miles on the beam, homeward bound, would suit him fine.

"Can't you smell this coast?"

The bo'sun told him that every coast has its own sniff, when you know it, and are near enough. That coast only smelt foreign to him, like their ship. That was all he could say about it. "You know, mister, when you've been away for a long spell, the sniff of the outfall at Barking and Becton gasworks, where your ship comes round on the hawsers to enter the Albert Dock at last, ain't too bad. Know it? But you don't. You haven't had enough experience of knocking about. It's London, anyhow. Canning Town is alongside."

"I know it," said Travers. "It's the same thing. It's knowing you have come to the right place. A cat has the same sentiment about a hearth-rug."

"Then it shows its sense, mister, knowing its own hearth-rug, and sticking to it."

Travers agreed. Even a cat must go by the signs which correspond to its ken.

"I've been this way lots of times, mister, all the same. I was along here on my first voyage, in the old *Zeus*. . . ."

"What ship, Bert?"

"The *Zeus*. She was a small steamer. I was only a kid then. We called at Syracuse . . ."

"I should say you did."

"What's that? I don't know why we went in there, not now, it's too long ago; and I've been here many times since. They're fruit ports here, and sulphur, and oil, and wine round at Palermo. In and out for years, but not lately. The women are pretty, but it's dangerous, this island. I don't see much in it. That coast is only something more you must be careful of. It's a bad coast. Give it as wide a berth as you can. I don't want to be near enough to see the houses."

"Well, to me it's like—what's that place you mentioned? It's as good as Canning Town."

The bo'sun did not answer that. Such nonsense ought not to be answered. Travers, unconscious of his folly, continued to watch the high land unfold. That glorious old fabulist Ulysses was this way once, and there was the panorama of scored ramparts he conned, while spinning lively yarns about the unknown to his men, to keep them going. His men were like Bert, a bit nervous; they couldn't smell their London. Their skipper had to make up his fables, because his ship was the first to lift those heights, yet he was not so far out. He couldn't have been extravagant enough to get near the truth; the bolder the guess the nearer the mark.

That land must have had the same countenance for Ulysses as it wore that morning. The mystery is always what it was. Let Zeus destroy your ship; the voyage of discovery cannot end, while the horizon lasts. Etna was still a silver cone afloat in the blue, with a drift of smoke in the windless air, a translated and dominating presence. How name all that, in the silence! He himself from those hills had seen Aurora come to earth. You must see it, to believe it. The gods live. They are born anew for all discoverers.

That land was dangerous. No doubt about that. Bert was right. It was highly dangerous. There was Etna, piled by Zeus over Enceladus, to keep that bold fellow under for challenging heaven; but Zeus was mistaken there. While the gods live, men will dare their lightning if it blinds them. Don't argue about it, but rejoice.

Bert took his gaze from a schooner inshore, that was diminished to a chromatic bird skimming along under the high quivering walls, and turned to the guv'nor to further his appeal for common-sense; but when he faced Travers he knew the guv'nor was alone.

Chapter Twenty-nine

COLONNA ITSELF WARNED OFF INTRUDERS. THE ISLAND, when first sighted, is nothing substantial, is not easy of belief. On the indubitable sea there appears, as faint and distant as the hope of sanctuary, a low cloud that does not move from the skyline in the wind. It persists, and heightens, and takes colour, but is nebulous land, perhaps is only a mirage from a legend, the forlorn dream of a disillusioned voyager who would escape from an insistent world, yet disbelieves there can be a landing-place. What he sees is only a private thought projected into a vision he will never reach.

Nor has Colonna a landing-place which may be trusted. It has but one, and that depends on the way of the wind. The island does most that isolation may to keep its secrets. It has, or it had, nothing to offer but quiet. For most of its coastline it falls sharply to the waters. The seas surge toward it, surrounding with white tumults outlying steeples and cupolas of rock, the perches of cormorants, to explode amid ledges and caverns that are unapproachable. Its upper slopes are for goats.

Colonna had nothing, you would have supposed, to invite enterprise and development. Its one beach for a landing is a brief shelf which needs a close watch to windward, and much local knowledge, if you would use the chance it offers. But not even an island abandoned as the haunt of old fables, where the only movements are of the surf about its rocks, and the shadows that creep round from the sun on its bare slopes, cast by the surviving masonry of temples to faiths forgotten, may escape, when it will serve as a useful step in the advance of important interests which know what they want, but are discreet.

Bert had gone down to Colonna's beach that morning to see what chance it offered. The sea was calm. The weather was settled. The opportunity had come. He shaded his eyes in the glare, trying to discern signs of a shoreward boat from a steamer anchored a mile out. She was half-dissolved in the radiance of the sea. There was no sign of a boat. No; nothing was doing there yet.

Just as he had expected, they were ordered out of that place. They were in the way. That fellow Quirke, whoever he was, was an ugly customer, and the bo'sun promised himself that if ever there was a lucky day in Liverpool, and they met in a quiet street . . . one minute was all he asked.

There was no signal about the steamer to show she was getting busy, so it was no good waiting. He would get hold of the guv'nor, all the same, and keep him close. The game was up, and they had better get out of it, while the weather was just right, and while the going was good.

The guv'nor very likely was taking a last look at his old stones. Bert surveyed the prospect, but could see nobody. Not a soul was about. The new jetty and its trolley line connecting it with the works ashore, was deserted, except for a man tinkering at a derrick with a mallet. That hammering was the only sound, except the echoes it roused in the hills, and the crying of a gull.

The beach was cumbered with hot boulders. Above it was a spread of rusty plants, thin and dry, in which crickets were whispering. Bert waded through it towards a new building that was near. Its red iron roof was a strange and conspicuous landmark, and cables radiated from it.

The herbage was strewn with empty packing-cases, parts of discarded machinery, and old statues and prone columns. He paused once to watch a circling aeroplane, which veered and sloped towards a rounded shed standing on a plateau above. Planes there, too? What was that chap after?

Well, if this place hadn't nearly everything! All it wanted now was a cinema. Even Bert's sense of the appropriate was jolted by that glistening machine in the sky. Somehow, even he could not fix it in his knowledge of seas where the ports were separated by days and much labour, and now and then a harbour must be missed because the wind is adverse. It struck him that in future there might be no more islands. An amusing idea!

He would go and stay with the electrician at the power-station, while waiting. He liked that lad, and from the door there he could see the guv'nor in any direction. Mr. Travers couldn't be far off. It eased the bo'sun's mind to be sure now that they could depart that day from a place where they might have been foreign spies, the way they were watched. Quirke's face wouldn't be the worse for a little shifting. You couldn't miss it, either. It had plenty of room.

The electrician in charge of the power-station always heartily agreed to that. That smart young Londoner, with his impudent eyes enlarged by goggles, his mop of hair as wild as a pianist's, and his white shirt and neat butterfly bow, was sure to grin broadly at any new definition of Quirke. When he himself had a few minutes to spare he could outline apt descriptions himself.

"There you are. Look here," he said at once to Bert, as the bo'sun turned into the house, "I've had a nice long talk with that friend of yours, Mr. Travers. I like the old sport. But really, what does he expect to do? Do you know?"

"Well, in a way."

"That's not good enough. He wants to save that temple, of course. So do I, but I happen to know we shan't do it. It's in the way. It hasn't an earthly chance."

"So I've told him."

"Is that all?"

Bert shifted a point, for he was keeping an outlook on the country, and faced the electrician directly, who then was not grinning ironically. He had a serious moment.

The bo'sun showed impatience. "Haven't you any sense, either? Can't you see that what my guv'nor says is just what he means, and no less? That is to say, if you understand what he means. Sometimes I don't."

"So it's true then," mused the electrician. "I was pretty sure it was."

"What is?"

The electrician tapped his forehead.

Bert was mildly contemptuous. "Is that all your book-learning does for clever young upstarts like you? You think a quiet man is not quite all there if he puzzles you. He can't be right in his head if his notion of things won't fit your tool-box. But understand that you puzzle him. As near as I can see it, he thinks you are crazy. How about that?"

The electrician fingered his bow, and adjusted his spectacles. He remained serious, and that was unusual for him. "All right, Mr. Byles. I won't say we're not. I've thought so myself now and then, when off duty, and fed up with this second-hand graveyard. I've been listening to your friend this morning, and I inferred, I just guessed, that we are certainly a bit weak in the head. It seemed to me that he supposes, in a sort of way, that we are ignorantly committing suicide, and what he is after is to save us. He has an idea that if we deliberately destroy that temple up there, then we put out our eyes. We shan't mean to do that, but that is what will happen to us. It seems to him that if we complete that ruin, instead of taking precious care of it, then hope for us is lost. We show we are the devil's own, or something like it. It will be a sign to the gods —some peculiarity of that sort. But he doesn't believe in them, does he?"

"He believes in something."

"He certainly does. He nearly made me late with a switch. He almost persuaded me of something, I don't know what. Pass over that bottle of beer. Where is he now?"

"I'm not sure. I should say he was up by the temple, or in it."

The electrician put down the bottle. He took out his watch. He stared up, open-mouthed, at the old building above. Bert followed his gaze. There it was, throned massively, white and definite, on its tawny hill. Its approach steps, colonnade, and architrave were as pronounced as a commanding call in that clear air. It was the mark of the island. It was authoritative and beautiful.

The electrician turned wonderingly to Bert. "I told him it was mined. Is he there? I told him, I tell you. He knows."

The electrician did not believe Mr. Travers would have gone there—not that morning. Not after what was said. Surely he wouldn't have gone to try . . . ?

Bert noted the majesty of the building in consternation. Was the guv'nor up there?

He was. Bert exclaimed, for they saw Travers mounting the steps. A fold in the hillside had hidden him.

The electrician, held by astonishment, watched till the figure was disappearing into the shadow of the interior of the temple. He cried out something. He sprang for the telephone, ringing it frantically. Nothing happened. He left it to dart to his switchboard, looking over his shoulder up the hill; but his hand was still reaching for a switch when the interior darkness of the temple turned scarlet, and the white masonry bulged outward in a black cloud. A flock of frightened doves hurtled seaward. A shudder passed through the earth.

Chapter Thirty

THOUGH AN OLD FAITH, WHICH WE HAD THOUGHT coeval with the rocks and trees, may fail at length to hearten us because it has not the grace to support our enjoyment of a new god; and though a day may come, and commonly does, when a revered symbol, signifying our admission of universal good, drifts away in the smoke of its dissolution on a wind of doctrine that has veered, there is rarely much to show for it. When events begin their work of change upon a familiar scene, they are usually as little noted as are those spermatic motes which fall upon the mind, while we are busy on important matters, yet presently develop into joy or woe. When the change is complete it is no new thing. It is the familiar scene.

A child stood by the side of the Serpentine, gravely watching the toy ships. Fanny Travers thought how lucky it was the sedate little figure stood straddling on uncertain legs between her and the sheen of the water. She could have hugged it. It might have been innocence on the verge, wondering at the splendour of its new world. Its nurse sat beside Fanny, sullenly dividing her attention between her charge and a magazine. Two elderly gentlemen, their hands resting on the heads of their canes, were at the other end of the seat. A matter of State had offended them. They shook their heads sadly over it because they knew that ignorance and corruption would not permit any change to come.

It was summer. Hyde Park was somnolent with London's immemorial usage. The attention of the child was not taken from the toys on the lustrous lake, nor its nurse from her magazine, nor the old gentlemen from their commination, to note the formation of aeroplanes which was flying over London. They were used to it. Fanny did not look for them, though she heard them. She was too affected by the delightful image of innocence posed soberly on the brink of lambent hazard. Then she became aware of the hour. She must go.

She made her way leisurely towards the Alcazar Hotel. At the gates of the park a man was selling the news of the day, and his broken hat was the mark of the importance allowed to those who bear paramount tidings; his placard, imperfect through neglect and weariness, announced no more than Crisis . . . Country Warned. Fanny did not see even that. She was anxiously intent for a safe check in the flow of cars in Park Lane, that gleaming tide of crystal and lacquer which proves the immortality of the life of the capital. Its pulse was easy, swift, and powerful.

She ascended steps between a parade of disciplined myrtles, and left the full summer afternoon to enter an imitation of cool romantic dusk within the Alcazar. It might have been the sudden lessening of the light which affected her, but her composure was disturbed, for a reason she did not pause to consider with particular care. She had heard much about this celebrated building before it had arisen, and that was not so very long ago. Not so long ago?

Now she wished that Mantell had chosen any place but this. Of course, he knew nothing about it, and she could not explain. No, she couldn't tell. It would be like a ghost story. It is never safe to try to explain a ghost story. And how odd! This was the first time she had seen the place! She had supposed it was like all other big hotels. The reality was unexpected. Something about it was unaccountable, but whatever it was she must get used to it.

Well, it was only her fancy. It wasn't the hotel at all. It was nothing but a little stir, a secret mouse, rustling in the silence of her own silly attic. The dust had moved. One's attic gets full of reminders—you don't like sweeping away even the cobwebs. In a forgetful moment she had lost herself among the cobwebs and the reminders. Really, nothing had moved there. It couldn't.

Or else, she reflected, she was little intimidated by the muffled secrecy of this babble about her in the Alcazar. What a crowd! And they were all so eager, almost excited. About what? For their voices were no more than the incessant whispering of a stream coming from you can't see where, and going to a place about which you know nothing. It was confusing. She would not like this building. It was outlandish. Those long mirrors with their prismatic rims, and the cold lights of mysterious origin, deepened vistas into the richly uncertain; she could see animated heads in the distance, afloat on nothing.

And those decorations! There had been drawings scattered on a studio floor—she had shuffled them out of the way with her feet. They were as private as an intimate voice in one's own house. Yet nobody else was looking at them. They were not there, except to her. She wished those distant pale faces, not clearly seen, in the half-light of the mirrored vista before her, did not so frequently change. Why were their eyes always averted? They never looked at her. Nor would she look at them—yet there she was, waiting to see whether the next hovering head in the mirror would be that of a woman or a man.

Oh, nonsense! She settled herself. She sat below the level of that magical mirror. She watched the passing of the fashionable throng. Was that any better? These people were noiseless, as if they had no solidity. How much was real of it all? A sense of its unsubstantiality, born of its subdued sounds, its original show of spectral wealth, and yet the usual appearance of the people who haunted it, disquieted her with a little fear. Was it real? And, if it were, ought it to be?

She hoped Mantell would not keep her waiting too long. She could not endure that place too long by herself. But of course he would not be late. He never was. Now the truth was, she told herself, it was those cold freakish lights, and the strangeness of the modern decorations, which gave her a tremor of insecurity. They might have been ironic. They might have been playing a game with everyone who was there. Somehow, the illumination of the place was a mockery; it had no heart.

She heard why so many people were there that afternoon. Famous Diana Lais, whose condoning smile, sweet and sad, is to be seen wherever there is a cinema screen, was to come presently to open an exhibition of Victorian wax-fruits. Wax-fruits were being collected by the judicious. Mantell, where was he? The music of the secluded orchestra chimed in with Miss Lais and wax-fruits. That music was harmonious with queer lights, and a mouse in the attic.

Fanny escaped with instant relief from the spell. There was no sense of insecurity about Mantell, when largely and abruptly he arrived, cheerfully pretending to be tired out, such was the heat and hurry of the day. At leisure, in well-merited ease, he took a brief survey of this novel saloon. His eyes fixed with a smile on one particular. He mentioned it with warm approval. Fanny did not look, for she had noticed it, and she did not answer him.

He leaned forward, and became serious and consultative. Had he better not go to look for this sailor man? This place might scare him off. It was time for him to arrive—that is, unless the fellow changed his mind about it. Probably he was a rough card and might change his mind at the very door, when he saw what the place was like. Wait a moment!

Bert Byles, however, was even then inflexible before

a magnificent but dubious doorkeeper. Uniforms never influenced Bert, who was giving a firm injunction as Mantell arrived. Not that Bert was sure of himself; the friendly elegance of this young man who greeted him only congealed him into a closer wariness. He was on his guard. There should be no trifling with what he knew.

But he was ready to yield to Mrs. Travers, when he met her. He saw at once she was the sort who should have anything they ask for, because they ask for only the right things, if you have them to give. But she was nervous. She hardly noticed him. He was sorry for her. Her hand was lost in a hard brown fist before she ventured a direct inspection of the figure which offered it.

This was the man, was it? What candid eyes, so bright and grey, and so deeply set in a head of bronze that it was as though she peered through them away into an empty distance.

It was empty; all empty space in that direction. She tried to speak to him, but nothing would come. He looked stern and immovable. She heard his voice, cool and deep, shortly answering Mantell—why did he keep looking at her, when answering Mantell—as if he did not want to say any more than he must.

What were they saying? The sailor would not sit down. Now he was deliberating, looking at the table, rubbing it with his fingers before he answered. She believed he wanted to get away from them. That was it. He wished to keep this to himself. It was his. He was brief and quiet with Mantell, as if he resented interference with what he possessed, yet supposed he must give away some of it, though it were wasted.

Mantell was being gently diplomatic, yet the sailor stiffened. "Eh?" he exclaimed. "You'd better leave that out. Don't you think it. He knew what he was doing. He always did. . . . Me? No, I didn't always see it, myself. But what's that to do with it? He knew, all right. What's more, he was the best gentleman I've ever met."

Mantell was kindly and courteous. The sailor fidgeted. He looked round; he turned to Fanny a steady appraisal, then hurriedly said good-bye to them. He blundered away.

Gone so soon? She watched his broad back till it was lost in the crowd. She glanced up enquiringly at Mantell. But he, too, was standing, gazing away as if taken by surprise.

Chapter Thirty-one

WITH HIS HANDS JAMMED HARD INTO HIS POCKETS, the bo'sun considered a square of pavement outside the hotel.

Now which way? The funnier the world the less you can laugh at it! People preferred to get things tangled so badly that you might as well cut them adrift; though it would have been easier to keep them shipshape, as well as more useful. That clever young spark inside wanted to hear everything, but didn't understand what he'd got. What was the good of talking to him? Never tell a man anything who is sure he knows.

He felt sorry for Mrs. Travers. How much did she know? Perhaps she knew enough. She had something to remember, so she was quiet. Talking doesn't help, if you know something you are never likely to forget. That makes a difference.

There was a difference. The shops, the traffic, the signs and wonders, Charing Cross, the Bank, rumbled at a distance; or, if they came close to him, they were a nuisance and in the way. He would have to get out of that. He didn't like it, somehow. You might as well try to be quiet with a steam-winch going. The sooner he was away again, the better.

On Tower Hill he heard the call of an outgoing steamer. That was right. It reminded him of work to do, and the guv'nor, and of the look of the sea in the middle-watch. Keep away from crowds; they upset everything.

There was a meeting on the hill. It had a familiar look to him. Some of that big bunch of lads might have been seamen, almost. They were listening to a man above them, whose hair kept falling into his eyes, to be thrust back again with energy; he was shouting at them, and sawing with his arm. Bert remembered that he had been in such a crowd himself, many a time. Whatever the trouble was now, they were pretty hot about it. Policemen stood around, taking no notice, their thumbs in their belts, waiting. The lads were cheering. He himself would have been cheering there, once. Now it didn't seem to matter; though it was not a bit of good telling them that, all the same.

Someone touched his arm. He half-turned. "Say, you're a seaman."

Bert measured his questioner. "That was a quick guess, my lad. If you go on like it, you'll be a cook's mate some day. But what about it?"

He listened patiently to what he was told, though he had heard all that before. He knew something more, now. People get what they ask for. It's no good grousing, when what you have asked for is on your plate.

"So," said Bert, "what you want me to do is to make more trouble? Not today, my lad. I'm making no more, if I can see a way to dodge it. There's enough in the hatches, without another bale. If I could make something else, I would; but what is it? That's the trouble I've got."

THE END

The
Snows of Helicon

SET IN LINOTYPE JANSON RECUT
FROM THE ORIGINAL MATRICES
NOW IN THE POSSESSION OF THE
STEMPEL FOUNDRY IN FRANK-
FURT-AM-MAIN. FORMAT BY
A. W. RUSHMORE. SET, PRINTED
A N D   B O U N D   B Y   T H E
HADDON CRAFTSMEN

Harper & Brothers
Publishers
1933